SMOKESTACK LIGHTNING

The son of a showman, Laurence Staig grew up among circus performers and fairground folk, first in Manchester and then in London, where his father ran a Wall of Death sideshow in Battersea Park Funfair. After graduating from Manchester and then London University, he was an arts administrator for a number of years, before becoming a full-time writer in 1987. He is a regular contributor to the *Independent* and the author of several science-fiction titles for young people, including *The Network*, *Dark Toys and Consumer Goods*, *The Glimpses* and *Shape Shifter*. He also plays blues and jazz guitar in a quartet. He lives in a village near Newmarket.

CW00796188

SMOKESTACK LIGHTNING

LAURENCE STAIG

WALKER BOOKS
LONDON

With much love –
for Babs Staig, my mother,
and the memory of Laurie Staig, my father

First published 1992 by Walker Books Ltd
87 Vauxhall Walk, London SE11 5HJ

This edition published 1993

Text © 1992 Laurence Staig

Printed in England by Clays Ltd., St. Ives plc.

British Library Cataloguing in Publication Data
A catalogue record for this book is
available from the British Library.

ISBN 0-7445-2379-6

Smokestack Lightnin'
Shining, just like gold,
Oh don't you hear me cry?
Whoo-hoo.

Tell me baby,
Where did you stay last night,
Oh don't you hear me cry?
Whoo-hoo.

Tell me baby,
What's the matter now,
Oh don't you hear me cry?
Whoo-hoo.

Well, stop your train
Let me go for a ride with you,
Well farewell
I'll never see you no more,
Don't you hear me cry?
Whoo-hoo.

"Smokestack Lightning"
by Chester Burnett (Howlin' Wolf)

CONTENTS

GIBBONS, AIR ACES AND HUMAN CANNON-BALLS

The gibbons woke me with the dawn. Their whooping cries would draw me out of dreams, teasing and cajoling, like a parent gently waking a sleeping child. I usually woke on my back, staring at the Perspex skylight roof of the caravan. To me, the gibbons chased away the night and welcomed the day.

I did not live in the jungle, I lived in the zoo.

My parents' caravan was sited, with other caravans, in a corner of Belle Vue Zoo, Manchester, near the gibbons' cage. The cage housed an entire colony of gibbons. It was an enormous square meshed palace of trees and truck-tyre swings.

Later in the morning, when the gibbons had stopped their display of vocal pyrotechnics, there were other sounds. Usually, while I was having breakfast, a rhythmic barking floated through the caravan window. A harsh-edged woman's voice joined in, crying out in a German accent:

"Here, Hans, here, Fritz! Come and geet your feesh!"

Soon the cries became a cacophony as the number of barkers grew.

"Oh, my beebees, give mama a beeg kiss! Come, Hansel, Wolfgang!"

I would rush from the breakfast table and stand in the doorway. Mrs Schmidt would be standing at the top of her caravan steps holding an aluminium bucket full of silver-flecked fish with huge dead eyes. She would throw the fish one by one to a crowd of black, whiskered sea lions. Occasionally one would flop back and raise its flippers in applause.

In the distance, wearing a white polo knit sweater and a peaked navy cap, was Captain Schmidt. Some way behind was a small army of more clumsy, shiny black sea lions, making their way towards us from the Exhibition Hall, where they lived during the winter months in a temporary pool. (The seals performed in the circus in the winter and in an open pool show in the funfair during the summer.)

In school once, we had a class discussion with the teacher about the different sounds that woke us each morning. Other kids talked of milk crates, slamming doors, scrapping cats, early morning buses and barking dogs. I spoke of caravans, singing monkeys, buckets of wet fish and barking sea lions. These were, after all, my neighbours.

I was born on 25 March 1950. Because of my mother's last-minute dash home to England from Paris, I just missed becoming a Frenchman. My aunt had insisted that my mother should have me delivered in a *British* nursing home in Fishponds, Bristol (where my aunt lived). I have always regretted that my mother made the trip – Paris sounds far more exotic.

My father was a fairground showman, and my arrival immediately curtailed my parents' travelling. So my father decided to put down roots in Manchester. My first home was Belle Vue Zoological Gardens.

It was a child's paradise, and not only because of the remarkable zoo. There was also a large funfair, an exhibition hall, a speedway and stock-car racing track and a world-famous circus. The circus was housed in a permanent building and opened in the winter when the funfair had shut down.

Show business was in my blood and I can trace my family's show-biz connections back to my grandfather, on my father's side of the family. He created the first Wall of Death, which in the early days was performed on bicycles. These were peddled at "amazing speeds" around a sloped track, styled like a modern racing track. Later, he changed the track to the more familiar "Wall", a cylinder around which motorcycles were driven.

Grandfather Staig pulled the entire family into the Wall act – my great-aunts, uncles, cousins. He went on to develop something even more spectacular, an extension of the Wall of Death which he called the Globe of Life. It was a steel lattice globe fifteen feet in diameter, and one motorcycle would loop the loop from top to bottom, while another would tear around the equator; they missed each other by inches. It required split-second timing, and was extremely dangerous. The act changed its name several times, to the Globe of Death, and later to the Globe Infernal.

Grandfather Staig also created the Australian Air Aces, a motorcycle-driven trapeze contraption, which was the talk of the showbiz world. My family were actually New Zealanders but they adopted the Australian tag to make the three A's. "The Aces" topped the bill at the London Palladium and the Paris Medrano, as well as variety theatres all around the world. The act was even chosen as a novelty feature for a Royal Command Performance in London. But the Command Performance never went ahead. The act was pulled at the last moment, when a nervous official thought the noise of the motorbike might upset the Queen. My father once told me that the Queen had been disappointed; I don't know if he was telling the truth.

My father, Laurence Arthur Staig (known as Laurie), came from a great tradition of Australian and New Zealand outdoor showmen. He was a stocky man who always seemed to have a twinkle in his eye, and a grin that would break into a raucous laugh without warning. Most of the time he wore a grey suit, with his hair brylcreemed back from a widow's peak, but around the funfair he wore riding breeches and a sports shirt.

Not surprisingly, I grew up with the idea that we were somehow *different* from other families. Even my mother had show business blood. She came from an ordinary working-class Bristol family, but she had trained as a dancer and met my father when she was working as a Tiller Girl at Coventry Theatre in 1942.

I never quite appreciated the novelty of our way of life. Later, when I went to school, I secretly yearned to be like my friends, who had houses or flats with proper bedrooms. They had a normal home life; mine was spent watching my parents perform before crowds of people, or being looked after by child-minders.

Camaraderie is strong in show business – it is as though you belong to an exclusive club. There was never any need for my mother to worry where I was, or whether I was safe, because everyone in the circus knew and looked out for one another. Before I went to school, my daily routine was being passed from "uncle" to "uncle". (In those days any grown-up was called "aunt" or "uncle", whether they were related to you or not.) Days passed with my time divided between the animal zoo and the human zoo. There were characters to be found in each.

Uncle Bill was the lion house keeper. He was a short bow-legged man with a large ginger mane who prowled rather than walked. He came from Bolton and often collected me to help him feed the lions.

The lion house was a huge concrete building not far from the caravan site. Tall bars stretched from floor to ceiling, and the walls were painted a bright desert-sand colour. Sawdust lay in uneven waves across the floor. It smelled hot and dry and made the back of your throat feel gritty. The lions' roars would echo up to the ceiling.

Bill took me along the back of the cages, where a narrow corridor ran the length of the building. From here chunks of meat, fixed to the end of spiked poles, were pushed through the bars for the lions to "paw off" for dinner.

If Uncle Bill looked slightly like one of his lions, then Uncle Arthur, the maintenance engineer for the fairground rides, arguably resembled one of his spanners. He was a tall lanky man who always wore navy blue overalls and a peaked cap. He worked from a ride called the Moon Rocket. At night the screams of thrilled fairground punters would echo out from within a circle of coloured lights which flashed around the ride as it hit top speed. This was the place to meet with candyfloss and toffee apples, where the noise of the latest pop records thundered out from aluminium speaker horns and the Teddy boys gathered to pick up the girls.

It was too dangerous a ride for me, it went very fast, but during the day when Uncle Arthur was checking the various mysterious cogs and wheels that made it go round, I was allowed a slower, private ride.

At midday we stopped for tea. Uncle Arthur had his special mug and I had mine. We would chat about the problems he'd been having with some mechanical part or other. I really did help. He once gave me the job of rebuilding a ball-bearing-based gear system. It was simple, but tricky, and I did it.

The Belle Vue site was owned by the local authority. Before you could operate your ride or other attraction, you had first to obtain "the concession". In return, Belle Vue would take a percentage of your box office takings. The term "Showman" (which my father preferred) was fading and being replaced by "concessionaire". Many fairground concessionaires came from strange and interesting backgrounds, not always from the expected showbiz tradition.

For example, to the east of Belle Vue Gardens, in a disused giraffe house, two ex-navy brothers, Lieutenant Commanders Ian and Brian Frazer, had installed a glass tank, like a giant aquarium. During the war their job had been to mine enemy German U-boats. They had been awarded the Victoria Cross for their missions.

They re-enacted their exploits in this tank before a paying audience. The Frazers employed my mother one season to provide the audience commentary as they performed inside the tank. I often used to watch the frogmen rehearse, but if they weren't about I would visit Peppino with his animals.

Peppino was a small portly Italian with shifty eyes and a reputation for meanness. He ran a small one-man circus in a curiously designed circular building to the north of the Gardens. There was something vaguely sinister about the building. The design hinted at medieval fairyland gothic (the kind of disturbing image that crops up in Walt Disney cartoons).

My father had previously used the building for the Globe of Death, before he bought a tent (so that he could also tour the act). It was built like a squat cylinder, with a castle turret-shaped roof above. I had always been slightly afraid of the place, for reasons I couldn't understand, either then or now. It was ideal for the Globe, allowing the audience to stand around the perimeter; but I would never watch my father ride the Globe there.

It was perfect for a circus, too.

Peppino was an "animal act" clown. He wore a red nose, white panstick, large toe-capped shoes, a chequered suit and a red painted bowler hat. He shared the act with a miniature pony and an assortment of monkeys and dogs dressed in little suits with Union Jack flags attached.

The dogs chased around the ring to "The Thunder and Lightning Polka", played on an old seventy-eight rpm record player. They leapt over one another and, eventually, on to the pony's back.

For me Peppino's little circus definitely had a dark side. Inside the building, shadows seemed to stretch further, and the crimson paintwork could shimmer as if it were a mysterious drape, concealing something else from our view. This place, with its strange turret and neighbouring glass-like boating lake, flickered through my dreams for years afterwards.

I have been fascinated by magic for as long as I can remember, although I cannot exactly pinpoint when this started. It must have been with the circus magicians, or the Belle Vue magician, Maskar.

I almost always met Maskar when he was in costume. He was billed as a Mystic, a magician "with powers that may just be more real than we imagine".

He performed in a small theatre near Peppino's circus. A flash (an enormous painted billboard that told you about the attraction inside) was fixed above the entrance, filled with the image of his face. He looked like a demon. Slanted, piercing eyes stared down as you passed by, and his goatee beard and moustache made him seem like a creature summoned from the Devil's basement.

I regarded Maskar with a sense of awe and wonder. He was a magician and he looked simply magnificent. He wore a turban with a jewelled brooch. His fingers were long and slender with immaculately manicured pointed nails, like a wizard's. He was dark and small in stature but had a magnetic charm on and off stage – charisma, a certain quality that set him apart.

For an hour he would mystify and confound you. He would swallow razor-blades and cotton, and minutes later he withdrew the blades from his mouth, threaded. He could eat glass, lie on nails, hypnotize members of the audience. He could swallow sparkling swords to their hilt.

I thought this man must have travelled to Manchester from a mountain top in Outer Mongolia, or at least from somewhere mysterious, somewhere dark and strange. (Perhaps he had come from a village in the northern reaches of the Khyber Pass?) I learned, years afterwards, that his duskiness was make-up and that he was from South Wales. Someone told me that Maskar's real name was Norman.

There were few kids about of my own age, but one day a new family arrived at the site and my mother introduced me to a German girl named Sonja. Her mother worked on a fairground stall, her father was disabled. He travelled about in what I can only describe as a motorized Bath chair. I learned that he had been a famous tightrope walker in a German circus, performing on a high wire without a net, until one day he fell and broke his back. He would let Sonja and me ride round the park with him.

(He wasn't legally allowed to take any passengers in his vehicle, so we had to hide under the long canvas cover that stretched up over the front section.)

A particular fairground stunt bonded our friendship. No matter what we were doing, Sonja and I would rush to the Sunday afternoon firing of the Human Cannon-ball. This was held at Belle Vue Lake, an artificial stretch of water with a central island. In the winter, firework displays and even famous battles were re-created there. I watched the Siege of Quebec once; it was a wonderful way of learning history.

The Human Cannon-ball was a free event that happened at three o'clock sharp. The Cannon-ball would dress in a silver suit and climb into a fat cigar-shaped silver cannon, by the side of the lake. A golden net was stretched across the bank of the island. Khachaturian's "Sabre Dance" screamed out of the public address system so that every punter's nerves were on edge with excitement. (It was also a piece of music that I grew to love with a passion. My parents hated it, my mother always claiming that it gave her indigestion. Whenever the record came up on Uncle Mac – the Saturday morning "Children's Favourites" radio programme – I would eagerly turn the volume up. My mother shot round the house, carrying out the housework faster than usual.) The climax of the "Sabre Dance" was the point at which the cannon exploded. A silver flash caught the sun as the Human Cannon-ball made a perfect arc into the golden flexing net.

Sonja and I thought that this was so incredible it

almost defied belief. On Monday mornings we threw stones into a net that we had rigged up between two of the caravans, accompanied by mouthed versions of the "Sabre Dance". That was how we played.

HOBO TOBY, POCKET WATCHES AND COBBLED STREETS

For the less affluent showmen (of which there were many, us included), the hard times arrived with the early autumn and winter. If the summer season had been bad then the problems were worse. My father had so many different winter jobs that I became dizzy trying to keep count of them all. He was, at different times, a baker, a taxi cab cleaner, a wrestling referee, a motor parts delivery man, a lorry driver, a fire alarm salesman, a children's entertainer – anything (within reason) which could earn a crust.

Belle Vue was run by an impressario called Sir Leslie Joseph. During the second year of our stay there, my father broke his kneecap in a Globe of Death accident, just at the end of the season. This meant that he would be unable to do any heavy work during the winter months. Sir Leslie Joseph asked my father if he had ever tried clowning. It was a job my father knew something about from an old Australian friend, a clown named Bill. He was also able to pick up tips from Uncle Sydney, a member of our family who had been a music hall comedian. My father agreed, and Clown Hobo Toby came into being.

Belle Vue Circus performed every winter, in a purpose built auditorium. Many international acts featured, often with exotic sounding names. A Dutch couple performed riveting escapology magic, the best I had ever seen. There were high-wire acts, with artists in glittering sequined costumes balanced dangerously above our heads on a twisting silver wire. Flying trapezes swung down from a dark and secret ceiling, and to the accompanying "oohs" and "ahhhs" of the audience, various contorted costumed shapes flew through the air. The famous Italian clown, Charlie Cairoli, performed one season too. The building shuddered with the roars of lions, tigers, elephants and, of course, with the barks of the neighbours, Captain and Mrs Schmidt's performing seals.

During the breaks between acts, large amounts of equipment had to be dismantled, and new apparatus reassembled as quickly as possible. Although the clowns had their own spot, their main function was to entertain the audience while all the prop-shifting was carried out.

The clowns were an anarchic bunch at Belle Vue, and they would rush out in groups and provide entertainment at various points around the ringside,

using the broad red top of the ring as a small platform stage. Sometimes they would wander off into
the audience and perform outrageous acts, such as
polishing a bald man's head, or sitting in somebody's lap, or producing a large banana from a
child's ear.

My father fitted into Belle Vue Circus like the
final piece in a jigsaw puzzle. The job offer from Sir
Leslie was simply "work to get by", but gradually
Hobo Toby earned a strange status that nobody
could have predicted.

Almost all circuses have their Master of Cere-
monies (MCs), their ringmasters. The Belle Vue
ringmaster was well known and respected. His name
was George Lockhart, and he was a portly man in his
fifties who said little but strode about, watching
the proceedings with the critical overview of a war-
lord. A submarine-shaped cigar – the same brand
as Winston Churchill smoked – always protruded
from his mouth, clouds of swirling blue cigar smoke
constantly catching the edge of a confusion of spot-
lights. He wore bright red tails, a gleaming snow-
white dress shirt, a black tie and a top hat.

George Lockhart oozed style and confidence. But
so did my father, and this was a quirky characteris-
tic for a clown. My father shadowed Lockhart, his
Hobo costume turned him into the ringmaster's
darker half. While the other clowns fooled around
and indulged in the usual slapstick, my father never
did. He was popular with the audience, especially
with children, and was always being booked outside
the circus for charity shows and children's parties.
He was given the unofficial role of comic MC.

Most of the clowns shared a single dressing room, but my father shared his with the entire Belle Vue Circus band, a collection of musicians who played in the style of such wartime dance bands as Glenn Miller. Their music was a constant commentary that propelled the performances, the percussion ever ready to tease emotions of excitement, fear and fun from the audience.

Hobo Toby opened the circus each night. He would stand at the edge of the circus ring opposite the band, who sat in a special balcony overlooking the ring. A trumpet voluntary signalled the start of a fast piece of music called the "Huntsman's Gallop". Etched against a solitary, moon blue disc of light, Hobo Toby would raise his arms and conduct the band – but using a ragged feather duster instead of a baton. This duster became a trade mark as well as a prop. Such an unusual and dramatic opening to the show made sure that the audience would remember him for the rest of the night.

Almost every night I was in the audience, but I watched from a privileged position in a balcony near the band. From here I watched my favourite acts over and over. As ever, it was the magicians that I particularly liked.

Although my father's stage presence was powerful, he was to me a remote, shadowy figure. My mother was clearly in charge of me. She was acutely aware that I was growing up in an alien environment and she was determined that I would not miss out on education.

I was taken to the library regularly and reading

became as much of a habit as cleaning my teeth. I was encouraged to read almost anything. I was bought a comic every day – *The Dandy*, *The Beano*, *Radio Fun*, *The Beezer*, *The Eagle* – and at Christmas I always got three annuals, and my parents' friends would chip in with Rupert books. Books were an essential part of life and they've remained so.

My mother read to me every night – and others were encouraged to do so too. Sometimes, after the circus was over, No-No or Whimsey Walker or other clowns would drop by the caravan. I was told stories by them beneath the subdued light and hiss of the gaslit wall lights.

Whimsey Walker lived in a polished chrome caravan just behind Mrs Schmidt's. One evening he invited me over. I had never been inside before and my jaw dropped when I finally went. There were clocks everywhere. There were cuckoo clocks with long-chained weights; circular chrome clocks in an Art Deco style; dozens of pocket watches which were strung across the walls as though they were looped Christmas decorations. Alarm clocks stood on shelves with carriage clocks, and there were novelty clocks with puppet figures.

I had never known of Whimsey's hobby before. A small workbench had been fitted beneath a series of shelves in a corner of the caravan and laid out on a black felt cloth were tweezers and tiny screwdrivers, brass and chrome cogs and wheels. He proudly presented me with a pocket watch and chain. I was thrilled to bits; it was, I think, the first "grown-up" present I had ever been given.

Later that night, fascinated with my new treasure,

I overwound the watch and was devastated. My mother told me not to worry, Whimsey Walker was, after all, an expert, wasn't he? The following morning, shortly after the gibbons' call, I hammered on Whimsey's door. A bleary-eyed figure with spiky hair in disarray stared down at me, as I held out the broken watch. Of course, he mended it.

Eventually, we moved out of the caravan and into a small terraced house; a two up two down with a backyard and no bathroom. It was straight out of early "Coronation Street", a terraced row with a cobbled street off Longsite, not far from Belle Vue. There was even a corner shop with a shopkeeper who was just like Alf Roberts. The address was Laurence Street, spelt with a U too.

The walk to Belle Vue from Laurence Street was desolate, even to my young eyes. We had to trudge across an industrial wasteland of bomb sites and derelict factories. It looked as if we were still in the war years, or even late-Victorian England.

It was easy to make friends, and the Belle Vue connection made me popular at school – although it never seemed anything special to me.

Many of my friends were poor, very poor. To my surprise I can still remember their names: Freddy, a little boy who always came to school filthy, wearing short trousers riddled with huge holes and tears; Wilf, whose nose always ran, who was constantly being reported for lice and had a similar dearth of clothes; and Sally, a girl who lived three doors down in a similarly sized house, but with loads of older brothers – one of whom lived there with his wife.

The rag and bone man came round often. In exchange for some rags he might give you a goldfish or a balloon. Freddy's mother used to give the man a large sack of rags, but only in exchange for being allowed to pick through the best of the other rags. We always knew when Freddy had a new wardrobe; he would turn up in the street, grinning from ear to ear with new rags and, if he was lucky, holding a balloon. I don't think Freddy's family would have been able to afford to feed a goldfish.

I have fond memories of our time in Laurence Street. There was a genuineness about the people in the neighbourhood, and although poverty was all around us, there was also much affection and warmth.

At this time I developed a great appetite for listening to the radio. I followed serials, such as *Journey into Space*. This was my first contact with dramatized science fiction, with amazing characters who had such names as Jet Morgan and Lemmy. *Paul Temple* was another favourite – an adult thriller – and *Toytown*, with Larry the Lamb and Dennis the Dachshund. And there were Saturday mornings with Uncle Mac and *Children's Favourites*. They were all essential listening.

We went to the cinema regularly, and this stimulated my imagination further. I became addicted to puppets. At first this was through a free-offer hand puppet rabbit, obtained by sending in dozens of vouchers from a spread called Magic Margarine. I wanted the rabbit after seeing one on display in the corner shop. My father complained for months afterwards because he had to have Magic Margarine on his bread.

As I collected more puppets they became the perfect vehicles for storytelling. "Uncle" Barney, an ex-Globe of Death rider and a carpenter, was even commissioned by my parents to build me my own private puppet theatre, which was permanently set up in the kitchen.

Then one evening my father announced that Sir Leslie Joseph had booked the Globe of Death for the Pleasure Gardens, Battersea Park, London. My father wanted to tour the show for a year first. We left Manchester and the circus and travelled. The Globe was packed into an enormous and precariously roadworthy furniture van, which my father drove.

I saw a lot of Britain. We played at such travelling fairs as the Nottingham Goose Fair and we even enjoyed a spell beside the sea when we stayed at Dreamland in Margate.

The reading programme my mother imposed was becoming stronger. I was accumulating a large chest of books.

BATTERSEA PARK, FLOOR POLISH AND DOSTOEVSKY

We arrived in London in 1957. Elvis Presley was riding up the charts with "Jailhouse Rock", while Buddy Holly's "Peggy Sue" could be heard on every jukebox in every coffee bar. Many things about London excited me, and I had been looking forward to the move. Here there were trains that ran under the ground, and you could go and see the Queen's house – Buckingham Palace. I especially wanted to visit Madame Tussaud's Waxworks with its Chamber of Horrors.

My mother decided to stay with a friend of hers in Harrow, while my father got on with the job of setting up the Globe of Death for the opening season at Battersea Park. I was allowed to go with him.

Being easygoing, my father wasn't too fussy about our accommodation and found us a grotty bedsit in Water Lane in Brixton. I enjoyed this brief period of adventure. We went out for breakfast, took trips to the cinema whenever we wanted to, and had fish and chip suppers out of newspaper every night. As a pair, committed to roughing it, we got on very well. I didn't have to wash the back of my neck before I went to bed if I didn't want to, and I could stay up late.

My first view of Battersea Park was on a bright spring morning. The Festival Gardens site had been built in 1951 for the Festival of Britain. Many rides were still to be assembled, and from what I could gather they were similar to Belle Vue's, but somehow tamer. Belle Vue had *two* Roller Coasters, the Scenic Railway and a notorious ride called "the Bobs" (speeds of a hundred miles an hour were claimed and none of the Globe of Death riders would go near it). Battersea Park had only one Roller Coaster – the Big Dipper, which paled in comparison.

The business arrangement was a similar set-up to Belle Vue's: showmen were contracted as concessionaires. To my disappointment there wasn't a zoo (other than a small children's zoo), but the park was larger and it didn't take long for me to feel at home.

Our show was in a prime spot. We had a permanent building opposite a ride called the Rotor. (This was a centrifugal drum, like an enormous spin-drier. The floor lowered, leaving the riders behind – stuck to the wall like flies.) To the left of us were the main turnstyle entrances next to the Haunted Mirror Maze.

Our building was a hollow pebbledash render construction, supported internally by a permanent skeletal framework of scaffolding. It was perfect for the Globe, although it was a favourite roosting spot for pigeons, who seemed unperturbed by motorcycle noise.

My mother arrived at the bedsit a few weeks later and was so horrified that she whisked me away, declaring that we would return when my father had found something better.

My father had always been pretty hopeless at the domestic side of things, and it was my mother who had to do the flat hunting. We found a temporary furnished flat in Wandsworth. This *was* an improvement on the bedsit, but not so much fun. Since my lifelong wish to have a dog could still not be satisfied because of the "no dogs allowed" rule in flats, I was given a budgie to shut me up. He was yellow, bad tempered with a vicious beak and I called him Tommy. I began to fill many exercise books with cartoons and stories about Tommy's imagined escapades. This was my first firm step towards writing regularly.

We soon heard that a more suitable flat had become vacant in Brixton Road, where my father's stepmother and aunt lived with my aunt's second husband, Syd Makin (he was the ex-music hall comic who had helped my father create Hobo Toby). Syd had managed to get us a two-roomed place at the top of the house. The rent was thirty shillings a week. I thought I had seen a circus in Belle Vue, but I wasn't prepared for what I found here.

I was the only kid at 321 Brixton Road, and that proved to be a problem, because everybody else was quite elderly. It was a four floor detached Victorian house standing back from the main road, with a semicircular gravel forecourt behind a crumbling brick and render wall. Stone steps led up to a portico and a pair of stained glass panelled front doors.

The back garden was a long tree-filled semi-wilderness that had been split into smaller gardens. These "plots" had been given to each tenant according to the length of time they had lived there. A grass-covered mound, that made the garden look as though it had developed a boil, rose from the centre. This was an air-raid shelter.

The inside of the house could have been the film set for a 1930s mystery thriller, or a Bette Davis drama. Stepping into it was like stepping back in time. The smell of Mansion polish rushed up your nostrils. Spiky, olive-green leafed plants stood menacingly in china bowls, or on bamboo trestle tables. The wallpaper was a thickly painted, brown anaglypta. Dark, highly polished linoleum reflected the few scattered shapes of daylight which fell either side of a long red central carpet. Then came a ballroom-broad staircase, with a gleaming chestnut-coloured handrail.

At the rear of the house, beside the staircase, a small lobby with a pay phone shone with the silver light cast from the rear garden through frosted-glass windows. Doors were kept tightly shut on either side of the hallway. There was a huge wooden board by the front door with sliding markers that announced whether you were IN or OUT. (This was supposed to be so that when the door was bolted last thing at night you weren't locked out, but it was really Syd's snoop indicator.)

On the first floor landing, Aunty May and Uncle Syd's flat was guarded by a crocodile skin, called Rufus. Like everything else, it was highly polished. The eyes were dead, but its brown stained teeth made it appear as though it were alive, and grinning.

My parents and I lived in two rooms on the upper floor opposite three others that were rented by an active spinster. She had once been an exotic dancer in a cabaret act in Holland. Her name was Gertie and she managed to make herself look exactly like Edith Sitwell: a hooked nose, heavy hooded eyelids and bunched grey hair. She would have been at home in *Macbeth*. Aunty Gertie, as I had to call her, was colder than Jack Frost.

On the first floor there were other interesting tenants. In the front room lived Vic. He was *very* "theatrical" (as my mother put it, but she actually meant "camp"). It was difficult to meet the real Vic. He was not only a master of disguise, but worked as a female impersonator in the theatre – a pantomime dame, and good at it. This was his main occupation during the pantomime season. For the rest of the year he worked in Battersea Park Funfair on the turnstiles if he didn't have any theatrical work, which was often the case.

Whenever I knocked on his door to borrow something for my mother, such as milk or sugar, he appeared in a silk Paisley dressing-gown. I could never understand why he sometimes emerged bald, or without any teeth, but I later discovered that he was a lot older than he looked. He had an array of wigs and spectacles and hats. I'm not so sure about the teeth. (He once provided our school play with an assortment of ladies' wigs for *The Importance of Being Earnest* when the ILEA supplies ran out.)

Just behind Vic's room lived Teddy, in a smaller but similarly styled bedsit. Teddy was in the same line of business as Vic, but was less camp. The pair of them had been pantomime dames in the same show. Sometimes arguments would break out about great female impersonators they had known and loved, who was the greatest Mother Goose and so on. Despite these eccentric traits, which I took in my stride, they may well have been two of the sanest and nicest people in the house.

A retired couple who had lived in the house the longest, since before the war, lived on the opposite side of the hall. Next door was a retired step-dancer – Aunty Dolly. Dolly, like many of the others, also lived on her own. Downstairs in the basement were other ex-theatricals.

During the war Brixton was renowned as a theatrical patch, and three theatres regularly put on shows, including the Brixton Empress (now a Granada Bingo Hall). Brixton had once had many theatrical "digs", and 321 was one of the leftover dinosaurs.

We encountered problems almost as soon as we arrived.

There were an awful lot of stairs and each flight finished with a small mat or rug. Like most kids of my age, I tended to rush everywhere, leaping across landings as door bells rang and friends called. It wasn't that I was an outrageous child, just active, and this wasn't liked by the other tenants at all. The floors beneath the mats began to be polished, so that

the mats slid easily. Lights would be turned out as I
made my way up or down the stairs in the evening.
Little campaigns began to start behind our backs.
Even May and Syd, who were family, began to regret
having "a kid in the house". Inviting us there had
been a mistake.

Urged on by Gertie, May would polish beneath
her landing mat with vigour. War officially broke
out when, after asking a hardware shop manager
what she could do about the problem, my mother
was handed a six inch nail. She took the nail home,
and hammered the mat to the floor that evening.
Nobody dared open their doors to check what was
going on as the sounds of hammering echoed
throughout the house.

The simmering animosity which haunted the
place was petty but wearing, particularly on my
mother. I grew to realize that gossip and conflict
were necessary to those who lived there, they
couldn't help it. On the day we left, Gertie hung a
large Union Jack out of the top-floor window while
the removal men loaded up the van.

I went to a small Church school, St John's,
snuggled behind the new Brixton police station.
Most of the kids were from working-class backgrounds, and they lived in high rise flats on the
estates or, like us, in private rented accommodation.
I liked the school a lot.

The staff were an incredible mix. The Head, a
red-faced man named Mr Noise, came from the West
Country. The Deputy was Mr A. E. Hackett, an ex-
military man who was six feet, six inches tall and as

impeccably dressed as a starched penguin. He sported
a military-style waxed moustache, with ends as sharp
as needles. Mr Hackett was feared, but liked. He had
a booming voice that would have been perfect in an
army exercise yard.

One year, I had a Welsh teacher called Mr Jones.
He looked exactly like Harry Secombe and had a
particular penchant for collecting cards from tea
packets, bubble gum packets, custard packets. You
name it, he collected it. He encouraged us to do the
same and then he would bring in his "doubles" to
swap. He was a big kid at heart. When I asked him
for his autograph before I left the class, he wrote
"Keep on trying".

His namesake, Miss Jones, taught us drama. She
was young and attractive but was forever pestering
me about my accent and striving to improve it, saying I had "potential". I wasn't aware that I had any
accent (or potential), but being from Manchester I
must have sounded different from the other kids.

My parents had recently got a battered television set.
It only received BBC, but television seemed a wonderful thing.

In common with the rest of the nation, I watched
an extraordinary weekly science fiction serial on the
BBC, which continued for six weeks. It was the scari-
est programme I had ever seen and had a profound
effect upon me. It was called *Quatermass and the
Pit* and it terrified the British public, who watched
it from behind their living-room sofas.

An adaptation of H.G. Wells' *The Invisible Man*
was another favourite of mine. I even wrote to the TV

company for a photograph of the star, and a postcard-sized picture of a figure in bandages and dark glasses arrived by return of post.

Whether I had been watching too much television, I don't know, but around this time I began to notice that I couldn't see the blackboard clearly. Miss Jones, concerned that my imagination might be fuelled by TV, warned my mother that I might falsify the optical test, so that I could wear "glamorous" film-star-styled spectacles. I failed the test and became cursed with round-framed National Health specs.

The Brixton Road house was only a short walk away from the school. My playground was around me. There were bomb sites all over the neighbourhood, and I belonged to gangs that might have been taken straight out of the William stories. We often played around the high rise flats at the top of the street. These were huge, ugly, housing blocks that backed on to Loughborough Junction. They are still standing. We played beneath the shadow of these monoliths, where the lifts always broke down. We became friendly with an elderly couple called Eadie and Fred, who lived on the *ninth floor* in one of these blocks. I could never understand the logic of that, especially as Eadie had bad legs.

Despite our problems at the house, it was a happy time. The school's association with the local church was a good one. The church had a Scout and Cubs Troop and I joined the Cubs. It was one of the most enjoyable aspects of growing up then. There was a real commitment from the troop leaders, and they gave me a practical and moral education.

My weekly visits to the library continued too. Our local library was the Tate Central, opposite Lambeth Town Hall, next to a flea pit cinema called the Pullman. The cinema was of particular interest to me because they were always showing X-rated films – American horror and science fiction. Although I was too young to get in, I loved to ogle the posters.

I joined the children's library. The librarian, Miss Janet Hill, was helpful and sympathetic to my search for "more interesting" books. I kept wandering into the adult library and she kept being asked to remove me. Eventually it was agreed that I could borrow adult books provided they were cleared by my parents.

I borrowed Edgar Allan Poe's *Tales of Mystery and Imagination*. I found some of the stories diffi-cult, but intriguing. I loved his poem "The Raven". I didn't understand a word of it, but I liked the sound of it. Other books I borrowed included: *The Hunchback of Notre Dame*, by Victor Hugo; *A Jour-ney to the Centre of the Earth*, by Jules Verne; and *Dr Jeckyll and Mr Hyde*, by Robert Louis Steven-son. My father was unhappy about my borrowing "Jeckyll and Hyde", but grudgingly let it go. These books introduced me to the great weird tradition in literature, which I discovered *was* respectable.

One day, while shopping with my mother in the Granville Arcade – a large indoor market off Cold-harbour Lane – we discovered a wire-frame comic stand in the window of a newsagent's. The stand dis-played a comic book version of Shakespeare's *Macbeth* in a series called Classics Illustrated. My mother bought it for me and when we got home I read it from cover to cover. A coupon on the back listed almost two hundred titles in the same series. I decided to collect them and eventually I built up a complete set. Those titles I particularly liked tempted me to read further and to borrow the actual books from the library. This was the idea behind the series; it's a pity they're not in print any more.

At Cubs, Akela had put me in for my Reading Proficiency Badge. Part of the examining procedure was to compile a list of books which you had read. I put down all the Classics Illustrated series, but didn't explain that they were comic versions. A librarian from the Tate Central was called in to carry out the examination. Three of us were due to be examined, and I was the last. The previous two kids had listed titles like *The Wind in the Willows*, *Swallows and Amazons* and *Just William*.

The librarian stared at my list in utter disbelief.

"I see you've read *Crime and Punishment*?"

I nodded.

"That's interesting. Who wrote it?"

"I can't pronounce it, but it was a Russian writer – something like Dostofski?"

Her eyebrows disappeared into her hair.

"Can you tell me what happens in the book?"

She sat in amazement as I recounted a fairly good, abridged version of the complex murder story. I must have come across as an extraordinarily precocious kid. Some of the titles I had listed were of very illustrious and difficult works of literature: *The Iliad*, *Ivanhoe*, *Les Miserables*, *Moby Dick* ... even *Hamlet*. She tried to catch me out – on authors' names or plot details – but I sailed through and passed. Before she went I told her that I liked to write stories and was writing my own version of *War and Peace*, and had she heard of it? Akela told me afterwards that she had left with a face as white as a sheet.

POP MUSIC, SPIDER LADIES AND BERT

As the sixties progressed I was drawn towards pop music like iron filings to a magnet. I'd always loved music, of every kind. Mr Hackett, at the primary school, had taken us to the Royal Festival Hall on Saturdays for the Robert Mayer Concerts for children. These gave me a good grounding in classical music. But I also loved pop music; there was something energetic and exciting about it. A dance craze, the Twist, had taken Great Britain by storm. It seemed that everywhere girls and boys were dancing – in the parks, at the fair. Pop culture was the first serious difference of opinion between my father and me. He hated modern dancing, and the music that went with it.

One evening, on the *Five O'clock News*, there was an item about "Walking Back to Happiness", a pop song by a schoolgirl called Helen Shapiro who was only fifteen years old. The record was such a success that she had left school to pursue a career as a professional singer. There was a film clip which showed her waving goodbye to her teachers and friends at the school gates. My father had to leave the room; he had turned a bright beetroot colour.

Popular music seemed accessible, within my grasp for the first time. I began to listen to the radio every Saturday morning when the charts were played and my father was out.

My father brought home a tiny portable radio and gave it to me as a present. The gift was on the condition that I listened to "the thing" in private, with an earphone. My radio was the fruit of a win he had on the "gee-gees", as he called horse racing. I could now listen to Radio Luxembourg, an all-night pop station – complete with atmospheric interference – beneath the bed covers. I particularly liked rock and roll, and sometimes there would be records by blues artists such as Big Bill Broonzy and Sonny Terry and Brownie McGhee, but at this time I only paid them cursory attention.

Around this time I became more active in running the business, too – helping to tear tickets while yelling: "Hurry along now please, the show is about to start, take your tickets, hurry along now please." There was also an interesting development in my father's career. He had grown tired of riding the Globe and as an experiment he split a small section of his building at Battersea and installed a sideshow called the Spider Lady. This was an old stage and fairground illusion. A huge spider's web was stretched across a grey cobblestone corner. In the centre of the web was a large spider with the living, breathing head of a woman. The spider lady was alive and would talk to punters who paid to come and gawp.

The illusionist who built the trick for my father, and who was to work with us for many years afterwards, was Robert Harbin. Harbin has been regarded by many as one of the greatest modern magicians and illusionists.

The show was a great success. It ran itself, although the problems of employing young attractive lady spiders was something my father had not forseen. (Many young men tried to become trapped in their web.) My father, however, clearly saw this as a chance to retire from the Globe, and in the years that followed we worked closely with Robert Harbin on a whole range of illusions. We never promoted the tricks as freak shows, as you would find in travelling fairs. We asked if you could "solve the mystery".

On Sunday mornings I travelled to Battersea Park with my father to watch and help as Harbin built his illusions for his TV show as well as for us. Robert Harbin's real name was Ned Williams. He wore a dark brown sheepskin jacket and always puffed at an enormous cigar as he worked. You couldn't help smiling at his enthusiasm as he shuffled around his latest construction, moving and fixing pieces of material here and there to decorate the web for the Spider Girl, or rearrange an exotic plastic flower, if it were Varna, the Jungle Girl. All the time he would be muttering, "This will be fantastic, bloody fantastic!"

He would pull me towards him to help when he wanted some item held in place, or as he knocked in a nail. At other times, if I had turned up with a friend, he would give a quick demonstration of origami (of which he was an expert) and hand over a quickly-made paper peacock, or rabbit.

We still kept the Globe and my father trained a couple of younger men so that he could take a back seat, but there were always problems of some kind, and it seemed to me that a future in magic was imminent.

My parents had made their minds up that when I went to secondary school, whether it was to be a grammar school or a secondary modern (depending on the results of the Eleven Plus), they would try to move house again. They thought that I should have my own bedroom, not only because of studying, homework and so on, but simply because I was getting older. My mother had put our name down for a council house or flat, but there was an incredible waiting list that went into years.

As usual, my father left this side of things to my mother, and through an agency she found us a flat in Berwyn Road, a little street around the corner from Tulse Hill in South London. We rented the upper floor of a 1920s semi-detached that appeared to be in the middle of being repaired. Everything was unfinished: the front garden wall looked as if the bricklayers had stopped for lunch; inside, the wallpaper only went round half of the walls and the odd door was painted with undercoat only. We should have heeded these signals, but my parents were desperate. My mother had been determined to escape from "321 Gothic Towers".

The accommodation was unfurnished, and the rent not too outrageous (rare in those days). It seemed that we had finally landed on our feet; we had found a "normal" house. Except for a couple of details, such as having to share the bathroom with the landlord, whose name was Bert, and the kitchen being so small that our cooker had to be installed on the landing, it seemed a palace.

Bert also had a cooker on the lower landing, one flight of stairs down, outside the bathroom. This was temporary, we were assured, and he was about to disconnect it. Bert seemed such a nice man. My father took him out for a drink the first night we moved in. He arrived home late from the local pub, the Tulse Hill Hotel, telling my mother that we had cracked it. Bert Westgate was one in a million, and wasn't it great to be living in a proper house at last?

Bert Westgate was, I suppose, in his late thirties, but he looked older. Lanky, with thinning hair, he had once been a professional footballer before a knee injury put an end to a sports career. He had the most strikingly bowed legs I had ever seen, and if his arms had been longer he could have passed for an ape on a dark night. Bert was a typical "sowf Londoner", a real lad. His trade was plastering (with some brick laying).

Bert lived in the downstairs front room on his own. He slept on a pull-down couch. When we were shown around the house, he maintained that his lifestyle was such that he ate out, or brought home fish and chips or a Chinese take-away, so he had no need of a kitchen. As we learned, the ominous cooker outside the bathroom was *occasionally* used, and the dishes were *occasionally* left in the bathroom sink with Bert's socks, pants or shirts.

The rear rooms downstairs were also rented out. These were let to a quiet elderly couple. They had lived in the house for about five years and were called the Huggetts.

One of my father's biggest faults was that he was content to put up with anything for a quiet life. A "softy" at heart, he was willing to paper over any cracks in life, provided everyone was happy. He also had an innate, and ultimately tragic, sense of trust. This is fatal in business, which is why he was a bad businessman. Where others heeded warnings, omens, signs, my father ignored them. If the Grim Reaper himself had stepped into our living room and declared "Beware", my father would have asked him to step out of his view of the television.

A condition that we were able to move into Bert's house was that we gave him one hundred pounds rent in advance. Bert, we learned, had debts. My father put this down to the stresses and strains of life – didn't we all have debts after all? One hundred pounds was a lot of money in those days, the rent was three pounds a week, so we were discussing almost two thirds of a year's advance. Bert's debts were mainly gambling debts. Since my father also shared Bert's penchant for putting money on "the gee-gees", he perfectly understood Bert's predicament.

Bert went through money as though he had his own Bank of England printing-press down in the cellar. He liked to go out and have a good time, and shortly after moving in, we witnessed the Bertrand Westgate "spruce-up" ritual, which was to accompany periods of short-term affluence.

The first and most dreadful thing that we had to put up with was the massive fry-up on the landing, combined with the ritual of washing and shaving, while drying his socks above the grill. A tour down memory lane with his vocal chords followed: Bert went through all Frank Sinatra's early songs, a few of Dean Martin's, and an occasional song or two (if we were lucky) from the current hit parade. Bert had a terrible voice, but to his ears it was a gift to be shared.

At first, it was funny.

The second part of the "affluent phase" involved Bert taking flight into the night, to return in the early hours with a young woman. One of these visitors, called Maria, was quite likeable and stayed for a couple of months.

My parents worried about the effect of this upon me. I took no notice of course. I couldn't understand the appeal of sex; it all sounded a bit silly to me. Therefore, when I knocked on Bert's door for a chat with Maria, Bert would nonchalantly yell for me to come in. He didn't seem to care, and it didn't bother me, that he was in bed starkers with a woman in a similar state.

My father always dealt with such matters in a protracted and clumsy manner. Later that day I was summoned to the table where he was checking his football pools. After a series of long sighs and embarrassed coughs he told me that there was nothing wrong with a man and a woman sleeping together in the same bed if they liked each other. The subject was approached with analogies to furry creatures cuddling up together in the wintertime. I just shrugged and went about whatever it was that I was doing then.

There were other reasons why Bert had accumulated so many debts. He hardly ever seemed to work. He was simply incredibly lazy. This explained the unfinished building projects about the house. The summer and spring months saw him reasonably active and he would try to rise by midday. When the winter months arrived we discovered that he was really a dormouse, capable of spending an entire winter in bed. I thought this was extraordinary.

Towards the end of the summer, I finally received the go-ahead from my parents concerning my life-long ambition to own a dog (Bert had said he didn't object). I didn't care what dog it was, as long as it had a black shiny nose and barked. As we didn't have much money the dog was going to have to cost next to nothing, and this ruled out a pedigree.

With the help of the People's Dispensary for Sick Animals at Tulse Hill I was given the address of some newly delivered mongrel puppies. I brought home a black and white mongrel, who I christened Sally. She cost five shillings.

When I presented the dog to my parents their first reaction was to stare at one another in disbelief. My father shook his head and said, "My God, we've got another child in the house."

SCHOOL CAPS, THE HANDS OF DRACULA AND JEREMY SPENCER

Strand School was hidden between rows of semis, halfway along a tree-lined road off Brixton Hill called Elm Park Road. Although it was a grammar school, the place had a reputation for being "a bit on the rough side", probably due to its location. The school, however, saw itself as an institution "in pursuit of academic excellence". Like most grammar schools, it was single sex.

It was in an old red brick building that dated from the 1930s. It looked like a huge house, made up from a symmetrical series of boxes, with a central hall that projected out to the front gates and a pair of double doors that nobody could mistake as anything other than the entrance. This was a feature of the thirties-style school building. (Most modern secondary schools, built during the late fifties and early sixties, were designed so that any visitors would have to search hard to find the entrance.)

The Strand was stubbornly independent, in its character and reputation. It seemed at odds with the clutch of other schools in the neighbourhood. Up the road, at the end of Elm Park, was Tulse Hill School. An enormous comprehensive which looked like an oversized block of council flats, the place was supposed to be tough. It was referred to, with some disdain, as "the matchbox factory". This alluded not only to the shape, but also to the supposed quality of education. Interestingly, I only ever heard this expression from the *masters* at Strand (as the teachers were called), never from any Strand pupils. The kids I knew who went to Tulse Hill were interesting, lively characters – no different from Strand kids. There was rumoured to be rivalry between Tulse Hill and Strand, with lunchtime fights and the like, according to the local press; but again, I don't think anything of the kind ever happened.

The thought of my first day at Strand School filled me with fear. It seemed a formal place. I had previously enjoyed quite a protected upbringing, with stints at lots of small schools. Although the Strand was nowhere near as big as some of today's schools, to me it seemed enormous. My mother tried to help by saying that I was going to have to get used to being a small fish in a big pond.

At the beginning of the summer she had been sent a long letter from the headmaster, explaining with pedantic precision school uniform regulations. Alongside lists of what one should wear, were lists of what one should not. The place smacked of regulation and discipline. "Pullovers of the highly coloured variety", were definitely out. Socks should have no trace of pattern. Shoes were to be of regulation style: no winklepickers (this was 1961). I was mildly surprised that there were no firm rules on underwear; I was expecting to have to wear the school badge, a lion, on the seat of my underpants.

There were other rules. You must never be seen eating in the street while in uniform. You must never eat ice-cream at any time. Sports and gym kit had to be of specific colours.

The school's biggest hang-up was the strict regulation that every item of school uniform had to be worn at all times. Even a missing sock could bring about a punishment too horrific to contemplate. This rule particularly applied to the school cap.

The Strand School cap was a typical schoolboy's peaked cap of the kind that is never seen nowadays. It had to be worn whenever you were anywhere outside the school gates. It was not to be worn inside the school. The rule was applied with a rigour worthy of the Spanish Inquisition. It was opposed by the students of Strand with slant-eyed, venomous hatred.

The first day started at half past one in the afternoon. This was a novelty for me, being used to school starting at nine o'clock, no matter what. My mother spent a long time making certain that I looked right; that my hair was the right length, that the crisp white shirt was spotless, socks the regulation grey or navy (navy that day, I think), and so on. And that the regulation cap fitted squarely on my unregulation head.

The route to school from the new house was easy;

school was a twenty minute walk away, up the hill from the Tulse Hill Hotel. That afternoon I set off early, briefcase in hand. In the distance other kids could be seen walking to school, and it was easy to distinguish the old lags from the new boys. New boys wore the cap properly, the peak pulled forward, squarely set above the short back and sides-framed ears. The older kids wore it more loosely, the cap bunched on the top of the head, or even balanced precariously on the back of the crown like a deflated beach-ball. I never worked out how they managed to get it to stay there; I guessed they must have borrowed hair grips from mothers or girl friends.

The reason behind the intense hatred of the school cap became clear when a crowd of sixth-form boys overtook me. They towered above me, one or two must have been eight feet tall or more. Dog-ends drooped from their lips, their eyes were set fiercely ahead, and they walked with a determination that could have earned them a place on the next polar expedition. I suppose the taller kids did look faintly ridiculous wearing schoolboy caps, but they were worn with a disdain that served as an outward emblem. It was their comment on Strand official-dom. They were, after all, keeping to the rules, and there was no rule that dictated the precise position of the school cap on the head. I thought this style looked mean, tough, perhaps even sexy to the local schoolgirls. I resisted the temptation to adopt a similar style, I was far too new (and too young).

About halfway up the hill I found myself gaining on a small squat-looking kid with a cap that was far too big for him. He wore short trousers (a dead give-away) and was struggling with a brand-new leather briefcase that looked large enough to have housed a doorstep salesman's entire range.

The kid had short red hair. A pair of bright red lips showed an occasional glimpse of semi-chipmunk teeth. His face was a mass of freckles. The briefcase was frequently swopped from one hand to another, and at times he even held the thing with both hands. This meant that he had suddenly to break into a sidelong sweep, almost walking like a crab.

I said "Hello" and asked him if he was new, knowing full well that he wasn't likely to be anything else. He replied in a strong south London accent, between cursing the terrible briefcase, that he was indeed a new boy and that his name was David Walker.

I walked the rest of the way to school with David, who told me, with a formal handshake, that his nickname was "Daisy". I didn't dare ask why; he hadn't turned a hair when he told me, and I had just nodded politely. I explained that I knew nobody at all at the school other than an older black kid called Milton (who I'd known from Cubs). "Daisy" Walker explained that a friend from his primary school called Keith was going too, but that was it. That was more than I had. I knew that Milton would be friendly and try to make me feel at home, but he was older. The butterflies in my stomach fluttered their wings.

As we turned left into the street that led to Elm Park and the Strand, a swarm of brand-new unmanageable briefcases and bobbing navy blue caps surged towards the red brick house. We must have resembled a flock of sheep, innocent as new-born lambs bumbling towards a new field, and then to what? Tall, officious looking boys who could have easily been teachers stood at the school gates with note pads in their hands. These were prefects, on the lookout for boys whose school uniform did not meet the prescribed description, particularly regarding the cap.

Some boys around me had defiantly not worn a cap, keeping it folded in their blazer pocket. Suddenly, it was whipped out and dropped on to the head, just before the gates. Daisy and I watched this with great interest.

At the school entrance, just in front of the main doors, was a blackboard. Neatly chalked instructions told first years to asssemble in the hall. We obliged, and went up the steps to the hall entrance.

The headmaster was an awesome and fear-inspiring gentleman named Mr J. E. Cox. He always wore a long black academic gown and, while he had a hard set jaw that closely resembled Desperate Dan's, the similarity ended there. His eyebrows were permanently knitted into a frown. He wore an immaculate dark grey suit with a white shirt that must have had a separate starched collar. As we entered the school, Mr Cox stood outside his office, beside the inner swing doors that led to the hall. Another first year, just ahead of us, an extremely small boy who also struggled with one of these oversized briefcases, made a thumbs up signal to the head while saying "Wotcha mate" in a voice so innocent that it completely disarmed Mr Cox, and made me gulp. Mr Cox said nothing, but I heard a gurgled swallow as I passed him.

We all sat at the front of the hall in silence. Ahead of us, with sweeping dark wood staircases on either side, was an oak-panelled organ, enormous grey pipes reaching up to the ceiling. Upon the panels, in polished brass plates, were engraved the names of old boys from the World Wars who had been killed in combat. Along the walls hung oil paintings of past headmasters. Unsmiling and severe, they stared down at us. I sat there in wonder, the pressure of history bearing down on me with such weight. I worried whether I would be able to take it. At the front of the hall stood several masters in long dark academic gowns holding clipboards.

Along the sides of the hall, rows of emergency double doors looked out on car parks and bicycle sheds. Through these could be glimpsed the rest of the pupils, making their way round to the rear playgrounds. Many of these kids stopped and peered through at us. One seedy-looking older boy was brave enough to run over to one of the doors and, after pulling a face at us, lift a sheet of card upon which had been drawn a skull and crossbones. A master saw him and raised his upper lip in a snarl. The boy grinned and ran away, hotly pursued by a prefect from the school gates. This was ominous. I shivered.

The Strand had a three form entry and we were to be divided into classes A, B and C. A master without a gown, who had a pale face with a skin that looked as if it had been powdered and slept in, moved towards us and introduced himself as Mr Voce. Mr Voce could have played the Joker in the film version of *Batman*. He briskly read the names of boys who were to be in his form – this was 1A. As we were brand new, it was thought kinder to separate us from the rest of the school initially, to be told something of Strand School life.

My name came up on the 1A list. Like lemmings, thirty-odd wide-eyed innocents trailed up the right-hand staircase behind Mr Voce.

1A's classroom was immediately to the right of the hall. We shuffled into the room, where rows of desks with deep grained wooden lids and ink wells faced the blackboard at the front. The master's desk stood on a small platform, which raised it above the others. This psychological platform arrangement was to be found in every classroom.

As we waited for one another to get straight, I saw that Daisy Walker was sitting nearby. He gave me a wink and then lifted his desk lid to see what was inside. I heard a gasp, and then murmurs of consternation all around me as others also lifted their desk lids. I did the same. There was a message written inside the lid in chalk: "Death to Weeds". Beneath this it read: "Tomorrow you die." I leaned across to Daisy's desk and read: "Weed killer – have some". A cartoon drawing of a bottle with a skull and cross bones on it had been chalked on the bottom of the desk. We looked at one another.

Mr Voce asked us quietly to lower the lids as he waved his hand dismissively. "Oh, don't worry about that, it's tradition."

Mr Voce was the nearest thing to a mother duck that a man could be. He taught mathematics and had always been responsible for the first form. Like most of the other teachers, he had taught at the school for a long time. He efficiently gabbled through essential pieces of information, which ranged from the geography of the school to the subject of our timetable.

The timetable was drawn on to the blackboard in chalk, with the help of a huge wooden ruler. Mr Voce pointed out that masters were known by their initials. This was another school custom. The Headmaster, Mr Cox, was JEC. Mr Voce was JKV, and so on. Mr Waddingham, the gym teacher, was HW. We also learned (but not from Mr Voce) that almost all masters had nicknames (that was a school tradition, too). Sometimes the nickname would appear from the master's initials. So Mr Edwards, the French master (TWE), became Tweed, a combination of his initials with his surname. Mr Voce was just plain and simple Jim. This really was his Christian name and reflected a lack of imagination on somebody's part.

Mr Cox was called by several names, but the one that was most commonly heard had a sinister ring to it, like the forbidden name of an ancient Arkadian demon: "The Hobbler".

Mr Voce gave us a potted history of the school. It was called the Strand because it was actually founded in the Strand, during the war. The connection somehow switched to King's College afterwards, and when the school moved into its own building, in which we were sitting, King's College Hospital was our adopted charity. Every Monday morning there was a collection for the hospital.

After copying the timetable, we were led down to the hall in a crocodile. We sat at the front, opposite the place where the school choir usually sat. The rest of the school flowed into the hall from either side of the memorial organ and through the double doors at the rear.

On the stage in front of the organ stood the deputy headmaster, Mr Phillips, a tall, elderly figure who reminded me of a grey-haired anteater. When the hall was full, a knowing quiet descended. The deputy head signalled to someone at the rear of the hall with a raised hymn book held in one hand. A bell sounded, and everyone around me rose to their feet. Jim Voce wrinkled his nose at us and mouthed "stand up".

Everybody's eyes were fixed to the front. I heard the swish of the swing doors as they opened and shut. I think there was an ominous draught of air. An irregular squeak and clunk followed. I peered to the left, over the heads of boys who were standing behind me. The partially bald head of Mr Cox bobbed up the central aisle, on course towards the front. He turned to the right at the head of the aisle, and paused at the staircase. He shot his arm out to the bannister rail and pulled himself up the stairs, each step creaking with his shifting weight. It had never struck me before but he had a distinct limp. Now I understood the nickname.

As the first hymn was sung I looked about the hall at some of the other masters (there did not appear to be any lady staff at all). Most were elderly, and all wore black academic gowns with fur hoods. I gradually noticed that many of the staff had obvious physical disabilities. There were several vacant stares from glass eyes. When I later saw the staff move around, several walked with a limp, like Mr

Cox. A few twitched. I later learned that there were more than just a few metal plates and false limbs. One master, Mr Sluce (nicknamed Slush), had a wooden leg, a plate at the back of his skull and a glass eye. He addressed us as if we were all in the army.

The school assembly was unremarkable. New masters and first years were welcomed by the head. Special notices were delivered and the entire proceeding ended with a rousing rendition of the school song: "Child of the Capital". We could only stand quietly and listen in amazement. It was a typical school song, designed to cause the breast to swell, to make you shed a tear. (I have to admit to liking the tune.) When school hymn books were issued to us later by the music teacher, Dr Fiddler (I kid you not), we were also given a glue-backed sheet with the words. This was to be stuck at the back of the hymn book for ever and ever. I can still recall the first verse:

Child of the capital,
Linked with the life of it,
Reared where its riverside palaces stand.
Playing her part in the stress and the strife of it,
Here's to the school that was born in the Strand.

My father kept his nose well and truly out of my school life, leaving it to my mother to supervise. He always appeared very preoccupied with the problems at Battersea Park. It had been difficult to run the Globe with others doing the riding. So, with great reluctance, he decided to sell the Globe of Death to

Vicki and Speedy (two of his riders) in Manchester. It didn't come as any surprise.

The partnership with Robert Harbin had worked well and so he decided to specialize in sideshows and to place a Spider Lady in Belle Vue with a manager.

My father had started to attract a small team of reliable staff, regularly employing actors and psychologists (who wanted to carry out in-depth studies of fairground business). A perennial employee was an actor named Paul Howlett. Paul demonstrated Harbin's greatest illusion, the Invisible Ray, which my father had first seen presented by Maskar at Belle Vue. Robert Harbin was enjoying a period of revived fame, having had several TV series on the BBC. The building that had housed the Globe was converted and divided into three. The larger space was fitted out with a stage for the Ray.

We promoted several illusions, but the Invisible Ray never failed to amaze the public. This was to be the warhorse of the Harbin-Staig partnership.

The audience entered the building to find a silver cabinet with rectangular light panels on the rear and sides on an otherwise empty stage. A member of the audience was invited to step up and stand inside the cabinet. Slowly, he or she would dissolve, as the rectangular panels of light glowed brighter and brighter. It was cleverly conceived, and it was difficult to work out how it was done. (The trick was based on a famous nineteenth-century French stage illusion called La Morte, and involved an effect of reversing light reflected on a special type of glass.) Because of the TV popularity of *The Invisible Man* series, we changed the name of the illusion from Ray to Man.

My father always asked me to design a flash for the shows, and to provide copy. Sometimes this would just be words: "amazing – fantastic – astounding – sensational – a mystery". Sometimes I would suggest phrases: "Varna the Jungle Woman – the natives called her Taboo!"

Our sideshows featured in several sixties British "B" movies and television programmes. They were usually worked into the plot of some seedy thriller, often starring William Hartnell or Sam Kydd. The Spider Lady featured in three episodes of *The Saint* with Roger Moore, and four episodes of *No Hiding Place*, a Scotland Yard police series. Media producers found themselves drawn to the fair for fifties and sixties London settings.

The illusions had their hits and misses. Harbin was used to designing shows for the stage – for a committed audience. The funfair was a different crowd altogether, so sometimes he didn't hit the right formula. "The World's First Captured Flying Saucer" didn't interest people at all. This was a space-station wheel which rotated effortlessly in space. It was obvious that there were no wires involved, and it was clever, but it simply wasn't sensational enough. Harbin later adapted this illusion and presented it to the Magic Circle as a piece for the Society's reception area.

"The Wowl" (half woman, half owl), left people puzzled. Again, this was clever, but seemed tame. "The Hands of Dracula", a pair of disembodied hands, emerged from a small coffin in a mad scientist's laboratory. Many members of the public considered this so uninspired that they demanded their money back, although as a trick it was excellent.

The British public were becoming hardened. Brought up on an increasing diet of clever TV and cinema special effects, it was becoming necessary to create more and more elaborate fairground toys. This had never been a problem with the motorcycle acts. Risking life and limb always ensured an attentive audience. My father's weakness was that he not only found it difficult to move into the sixties and identify new trends, he hated and resisted the changes that were happening around him. It became increasingly apparent that he could not understand what was happening, and had no desire to learn.

Friends from school would come along at weekends to work on the shows. Several mates spent hours sitting behind a pair of mirrors with their hands pushed into rubber gloves, thus becoming the Hands of Dracula. Others would operate the Invisible Man illusion next door.

My father never seemed to be about, but there were several bars in the park that I began to have to check out if he was wanted urgently. He didn't drink a great deal, but he did drink to escape the responsibility of the shows. His liking for gambling also grew. Gradually and reluctantly I took over his role as a supervisor at weekends and holidays.

I wasn't doing very well at school, and it wasn't because I was stupid. I just couldn't seem to remember facts, and the grammar school education was orientated towards feats of memory instead of problem-solving. My own story-writing didn't seem to interest anybody, and if I was caught writing a story during a free period I was told to get on with some *serious* work.

I became friendly with a small gang of boys who were outside the accepted norm of the Strand school-boy: "Daisy" Walker, his primary school friend, Keith Wood and two other boys, Bob West and David Catchpole.

Bob West was cunningly subversive, reserved, and seemed a bit slow, but was in fact bright (if bonkers). He was a tall, soft-spoken kid who was growing long hair. (The Beatles and the Rolling Stones were fast becoming popular, but I think he also wanted to hide a pair of Prince Charles ears.) He shuffled about with his head drooped and his tie halfway round his neck. Bob was terribly lazy, and he liked nothing better than to cause as much chaos as possible during lessons.

David Catchpole was a small, beaming kid who always seemed happy, but was picked on by every-body because of his philosophical approach to life. If his hat was nicked by an older kid, or his bag was thrown on to the gym roof, he would try to reason and philosophize about the sense of these actions. He might have made a good negotiator with proper training, but his logic was confused, and he deliv-ered his argument with such a pompous air that everyone about him collapsed into laughter. Even the teachers found it hard to resist having a go at him. For reasons I cannot explain (there probably weren't any), Bob nicknamed David "Fido" (or Fide for short).

The fringe comedians – Peter Cook and Dudley Moore in particular – had become very popular, and we fell into the art of impersonation easily. Funny voices reigned at school, and we used to experiment by calling out unusual words such as "Aardvark" or "Genuflect", in strange elongated accents. We rejoiced for weeks afterwards when, during a geography lesson, we were acquainted with "Delta of the Rhone". Spoken in a nasal voice at speed, the innocuous German river acquired a new character – "Delta-of-the Rhooooon".

The four of us were quite different, but although we had our ups and downs we stayed together. We all shared an interest in art, but there was also a growing and significant interest in the Rolling Stones' music – not just the personalities, the actual sounds. Bob West and "Daisy" knew far more about the origins of rhythm and blues (R&B) than the average fan. They spoke of such strangely named musicians as Sonny Boy Williamson and Muddy Waters. I became interested too (I have always been inquisitive about the origins of things). I was really getting into the Stones.

The art of impersonation ran rife at the Strand. It was not simply because the teaching staff were so easy to take off, a genuine talent for wry comedy and wit ran through many pupils. The headmaster was a favoured victim. He had many quirky mannerisms, one of which was to yell down the corridor a war cry of "I'll have that boy!" in a voice that would curdle the blood. He would then propel himself towards the poor unfortunate, who had either frozen to the spot with fear or, if he were wise, made a dash for it.

A particularly small kid, who looked like a first year but who was really a third, kept attracting large crowds around him. His name was Jeremy Spencer, and he was able to bring the entire rear playground to a standstill by his astoundingly accurate impersonation of the headmaster. Crowds would quickly gather round him and he would rise to the occasion. Once he had managed to get into his stride so well, that the window of the staff room, above the rear playground, was raised, and a senior teacher had to bring a halt to the show.

Jeremy was very musical. A leading light of the school orchestra, he played the violin, the clarinet and the piano. He also did impressions of great rock and roll singers, Jerry Lee Lewis and Elvis Presley in particular. He went on to develop slide or bottleneck guitar, a style of playing that had begun to fascinate me (a metal or glass tube is slid along the strings). One of the greatest exponents of this style was the late Elmore James, who Jeremy could also impersonate with startling accuracy.

After he was expelled for impersonating the headmaster once too often, Jeremy Spencer moved to Birmingham. He returned later to become one of the founder members of Fleetwood Mac, a band whose first incarnation had many associations with our circle of friends. Blues circles were incestuous and small. Jeremy became legendary for resurrecting the Elmore James style. With guitarist Peter Green, Jeremy brought his repertoire of rock impressions into Fleetwood Mac's stage act. I think he even did one of the headmaster when they appeared at the Albert Hall in 1969.

TV SCRIPTS, DENNIS WHEATLEY AND WALKING STICKS

Malcolm (or M. R. Saunders) was a boy who lived round the corner from Berwyn Road, in one of a small parade of half a dozen shops on the High Street. His parents used the shop as an office rather than a retail outlet. A solitary bathroom sink stood in the front window against which was propped a sign that read: A. E. SAUNDERS, BUILDERS.

Malcolm was a friend of John Yates, a boy who lived opposite me. When I first arrived at Berwyn Road they were wary of talking to me, just giving polite nods instead. When one day they did finally introduce themselves it was carried off very formally. Malcolm presented himself as Malcolm Raymond Saunders – M. R. Saunders. I thought this an odd way to start, but I put it down to his father being

known as A. E. Saunders. I introduced myself as
Laurence, adding L. F. Staig or Laurence Frederick
Staig if he wanted to know my full name.

Malcolm was tall, but walked with a stoop so that
his shoulders appeared suspended on strings like a
puppet's. He had dark hair, freckles and an aqualine
nose that wasn't quite a hook but looked as if it
wanted to be. There were common points that drew
us together very quickly and we became firm
friends. Malcolm, like myself, was an avid reader,
and had an enormous collection of books. We both
liked H. G. Wells and Jules Verne, and he had also
grown up reading Classics Illustrated, the comic
series. But there was more. I told him about my writing, that I had filled volumes of exercise books with
stories of Tommy the Budgie. Malcolm had appar-
ently done something similar with his own cartoon
character. He was also halfway through a novel! That
piece of information floored me. An actual *novel*! He
showed it to me, a meandering scrawl written scruff-
ily in several shades of biro in all manner of different notebooks. It was a science fiction story called
"Back Beyond the Link", a brilliant title, I thought.

Not only was I impressed, but the notion that
another kid had pulled himself out from the child-
ish comic strip approach to writing that I had been
carrying on with, encouraged me to take a new direction. I forgot that he was a couple of years older.
That evening the Tommy stories ended. I was going
to *grow up*, I decided. From now on I would write
lengthy prose; the days of my scribbled illustration
would be no more.

I had recently bought a copy of the script to Nigel

Kneale's TV serial *Quatermass and the Pit*. It had been published as a Penguin paperback, and I read it that night from cover to cover.

The next day was a Saturday, and that morning, sitting at the dining-room table, I started my own version of a Kneale SF TV serial: "Contact with Vongberd". This was an important step forward. I noted that in the Penguin book Kneale had left camera instructions such as *fade to black, pan in, dissolve, crash in music.* I used these in my own script.

Malcolm walked to school each morning past Brockwell Park, the same park where I used to take Sally for a walk. We met each morning and gave each other updates on writing. He prompted me to stick with it, and I'm sure that I had a similar effect on him. He became very taken with the playscript approach.

We met three or four times a week at each other's houses. Sitting face to face, across a small card table, we would churn out pages of playscripts. Each had its own cover, drawn and coloured in with crayon and pencil. We wrote dozens and dozens, we became writing machines, as active as a pair of hungry Hollywood scriptwriters.

Other kids found it difficult to understand why on earth we did this: "What do you mean you sit opposite one another and write?"

When an episode had been written, we would read it aloud.

This small but industrious two-hand writer's circle was fuelled and inspired by our competitive reading. On Saturday mornings we would visit W. H. Smith in Streatham to peruse the paperbacks and buy a

book. Each month we went to Charing Cross Road
to look at the hardback copies of Dennis Wheatley's
and Ian Fleming's books, and sometimes we would
buy one if we had saved enough pocket money.
Books were one of the most important things in our
lives. We even made up *Top Tens* every month and
produced a literary supplement for friends.

Gradually, under the influence of Dennis Wheatley and his character the Duc de Richleau, we
created similar characters of our own: Malcolm had
Sir John Shep, and I had Sir Richard Garn. Garn
had featured in my first play, "Contact with Vongberd", but he didn't have a knighthood then.
Malcolm had always had a snobbish streak in him,
and so not to be left out, Richard Garn acquired a
knighthood too.

Inspiration worked at full power then; we
responded to anything that we read in a book. Eventually, the fantasy spilled into the real world.

The first blurring of fantasy and reality was fairly
harmless. Most kids have secret clubs and gangs,
often imitating William's Outlaws or Enid Blyton's
Secret Seven. I'm not sure that we were cast from
the Secret Seven mould.

Around the corner from where I lived was an old
derelict house. Set back from the High Street, it
stood in a jungle of a garden. It was known as
Hobo's Hotel because tramps used to stay there
occasionally. The place hadn't been touched for
years, and sheets of newspaper with headlines about
the war could be found under the lino or stuck in
cupboards. John and Malcolm decided that this was
to be our base, with a "hide-out" down in the cellar.

John decided, with a touch of irony (I think), that he was to be known as "The Bloody Skull", and the club itself was christened "The Three O'clock Club". In theory, this was to be the time when we would slip out from our beds and meet. (I only ever managed to get out of the house once, the first night.) John was to go ahead and prepare the cellar, with candles and late night snacks. Malcolm had bought a pipe and a walking stick as accessories to initiate the first meeting.

At three o'clock in the morning the world is as silent as the grave. Sometimes called the "Hour of the Wolf", it is reputedly the time when most people die and most babies are born. Dreams are at their most powerful and the life force is at its lowest ebb. That suited us perfectly. The streets were deserted, the only sounds were those of scrapping cats.

When Malcolm and I arrived at the house, there was no sign of John. Boxes of candles lay on the wine cellar shelves, so we fixed ourselves up with a makeshift light of dozens of tiny flames. I volunteered to go and check on John, Malcolm apprehensively agreed to wait.

Going back through the house alone was nerve-racking. I was certain that I saw faces peering at me from every corner, beneath every shadow. I was glad not to be in Malcolm's place, alone in the cellar.

I met John at the bottom of Berwyn Road. He had overslept and found it difficult to creep out. "The Bloody Skull" looked very uncertain about his role in all this and kept yawning. We sneaked back into the front garden of Hobo's Hotel, but stopped as we approached the stone steps that led up to the front entrance. The door was open wide. The outline of a dark shadowy figure stood in the hallway. After a moment we realized it was Malcolm, with the walking stick held defensively, like a club. An exchange of whispers reassured him that it was us.

When we joined Malcolm in the hallway my torch revealed an ashen face, with frightened eyes. His pipe had gone out and hung limply from the side of his mouth.

"In the cellar," he said slowly, in a hushed voice. "I saw it, a face, it was horrible – and it went right through the wall."

We exchanged glances. The Bloody Skull gulped, and said he wanted to go home.

Malcolm's father had done well in the building-trade boom of the early sixties. Alf specialized in the conversion of West End/Soho buildings into coffee-houses. These were popular in the sixties. He had built some of the most famous: Le Macabre Coffee House, which had coffins for tables and benches, and the Cromwellian Club, in Kensington (an overnight "Bonnie and Clyde" styled conversion, commissioned when the Warren Beatty film became a hit). This boom meant that the Saunders family were able to buy a beautiful semi off Red Post Hill. This took Malcolm from my immediate neighbourhood, but we remained in contact; it was only a short bus ride.

Malcolm's new house had a long garden, the bottom of which was screened by a wooden trellis. I was urgently called over to Malcolm's one morning and led to the bottom of the garden. He had started work on digging a trench behind the trellis.

"I'm making a mole machine," he announced in a matter-of-fact manner. "I need you to help me design and make the costume."

I had no idea what a mole costume should look like. I wasn't any good at sewing. I think he simply needed moral support.

Like Daedalus, there were always flaws in Malcolm's inventions. He had calculated that it should be possible, with the aid of a pair of small potting trowels, to dig down into the bowels of the earth. I immediately saw problems with this, but he wouldn't have any of it. I went along for fun. (He was so adamant that it was going to work that he required a suit *before* any trials.)

We adapted some old clothes, and I managed to sew together a hood to keep the vast quantities of soil that would be removed out of his hair. His parents had no idea what we were doing. When he was finally dressed and ready I lowered him into the trench by his ankles and handed him the "special" pair of trowels.

It was a very funny sight. Scuffles of dirt were flung into the air, only to land back in the hole again. The sounds of spluttering and swearing mixed with moans and grunts.

Ten minutes later, when I pulled a panting Malcolm from the trench, he declared that perhaps it wasn't such a good idea after all. We decided to cover the hole up temporarily with leaves, the idea being we would convert it to a nuclear fallout shelter later.

Ideas for inventions tumbled fast and furiously.

We read a famous theoretical book about time travel
– J. W. Dunne's *An Experiment With Time* – in the
reference library at the Tate Central.

The book arrived. There was a stern expression on
the librarian's face. "Don't believe everything you
read in this, OK?" She warned us.

We nodded, but Malcolm did believe and had
developed ideas of his own.

I cannot recall all the thinking, the vast Einstein-
ian theories that contributed to Malcolm's theory of
time travel, but he was convinced that it *was* possible. The worrying thing was that one aspect of the
theory required the subject to be wired up to a truck
battery.

I ended up sitting in the Saunders' kitchen one
evening when his parents had gone out. I had the
wires taped to my temples. (Do NOT try this at
home.) Glasses of water were placed in front of me,
into which I dipped my fingers. The wires continued
down to a large battery, freshly charged.

Later, after a cup of coffee had steadied my nerves
and the tingling sensation in my head had cleared,
Malcolm agreed that perhaps the time travel theory
wasn't right and needed modification.

Shortly after this, we tried to make his bicycle
into a man-powered flying machine with the aid of
strategically attached umbrella's. Malcolm's neighbours came out of their houses to watch as we cycled
up and down the road, umbrella's flapping like
demented bat wings. It nearly worked, but not
quite.

Matters reached a head when Malcolm's father fell
down the trench-cum-nuclear fallout shelter, buried

beneath the leaves. He had been innocently pruning the roses.

This was the end of our period of inventions. In their place we discussed the mysteries of sex. I was still nonplussed by it all, despite having learnt about the birds and bees several years earlier from my mother one lunch-time.

I had called home from school. I had been having an argument with an older boy who declared that there was no such thing as Father Christmas and fairies and so on. This was rubbish; of course these creatures existed. My mother, taking a deep breath, gave me the lot – the facts – all at one go. I was mortified. No tooth fairy? No white bearded benefactor, and men and women do what?! It sounded hilarious. My father was very quiet when he came home later that night, eyeing me suspiciously out of the corner of his eye. I'm not sure that he had approved of my mother telling me everything.

A new "seriousness" entered our writing. We stopped writing TV scripts with cartoon covers and both began to write novels with chapters. These were scribbled into exercise books. We still met to write together and Dennis Wheatley and Ian Fleming were still major influences, but we were reading more widely too. I had started to read Ray Bradbury's books at the suggestion of a local librarian. *The Golden Apples of the Sun* was the first. I went on to read stories by Arthur C. Clarke and Frederic Brown. We both loved anything by H. G. Wells, who we regarded as the master.

My attempted novels had titles such as: *This World Does Not Exist* (fantasy), *Seven Sought Sanc-*

tuary (about mad scientists in Siberia), *The Valley of the Valhalla* (based on Wagner's Ring Cycle – Malcolm and I both loved Wagner) and *As Far As We Can Go* (an SF story about time reversal). Malcolm's titles were similar: *Trespassers Will Be Prosecuted* (after Wheatley's *The Forbidden Territory* – we were very taken with the idea of Russian Agents), *The Eating Planets* and so on. We even co-wrote a novel, *The World Awaits*, working on alternate chapters and enjoying writing each other into tight corners.

My parents were beginning to wonder how much longer they could put up with living in Berwyn Road. Life there was becoming wilder.

The elderly lady in the flat downstairs had taken to serious drinking, partly because of Bert, and underwent periods of complex hallucination. This involved much ranting and raving, and effing and blinding.

That winter Bert had entered a long and dedicated period of hibernation – his best yet. He also sublet the stairs, cellar and landing to four labourers from Dublin, who camped out in sleeping bags. Occasionally, they would all rise together, like the awakening of the Living Dead in George Romero's Zombie movies. We were treated to medleys never heard by human ears before. The usual Frank Sinatra songs would jostle with tear-jerking versions of "Danny Boy" and the "Lonesome Boatman", as socks were dried above the grill and fry-ups were cooked on the greasy stove. Thus fed, they would consume several bottles of Guinness before climbing back into the bags. This was probably the straw that broke the camel's (my mother's) back.

We decided to move.

Again it was down to my mother to find us somewhere. Unfurnished places were still rarer than hen's teeth, and we were number 5001 on the council waiting list. Then a self-contained flat was advertised in the local paper. As nothing in our lives had ever been straightforward, the flat was, of course, far from perfect. There was also the catch that we had to buy "fixtures and fittings" from the previous occupant at an inflated price, but my mother didn't care.

The flat occupied the middle of three floors in a converted pub in Birkbeck Place, a side road off Thurlow Park Road, just around the corner from the Tulse Hill Hotel. The bonus point was that it was self-contained. Privacy. There would be no more songs from Bert, and no more bodies to step over.

Since the building had been a corner pub, built on an acute bend, none of the rooms were of a regular size. They were a mixture of geometrical shapes – trapeziums, octagons, parallelograms. Even the stairs were set at an angle. There was only one bedroom too, so I would have to sleep on the couch.

My spell as an occupant of the couch didn't last long. I was getting more and more homework, and my mother was still set on the idea that I should go on to college when I left school. After several months we swapped. My parents bought a large bed that folded up into the wall, and I moved into their room.

This move enabled me to create my own study

and it also gave me some much desired privacy. I had appeared on a television quiz game programme called *Criss Cross Quiz*. The show was a general knowledge quiz based on noughts and crosses, and had been around for years. I managed to remain champion for a nervous, uncertain three weeks, which gave me enough points to get a much coveted prize – a Decca record player.

We had never had a phone of our own before, and my father decided to keep the one that came with the flat, declaring that it would be useful for business. (I could never understand how he had managed without one.) And it was located in the bedroom, which was now *my* room.

There was a single charge for local calls, then. So you could talk for hours if you wanted to, for threepence. Malcolm and I used the telephone to carry out gags on unsuspecting London telephone subscribers.

We developed a particular predilection for phoning people with titles. There was one gentleman – Sir John Bigsby-Edwards, who lived in St John's Wood – who was the unfortunate subject of several of our calls. He sounded exactly like a Dennis Wheatley character. Malcolm would call Sir John and introduce himself as "Brand of the Yard". The announcement would be made brusquely, as we had observed in Edgar Wallace *Man of Mystery* thrillers at the cinema.

"Yes, Inspector Brand, how can I help you?"

"Sir John, we thought we had better inform you of a confidence trickster who has been operating in your neighbourhood."

"Good heavens, you don't say!"

"There's no need to be alarmed, Sir John. He's an Italian. A small-time crook called Mr Elio. He'll call you and tell you that you've won a mural for your bathroom. He'll ask if he can come round to measure up."

"You don't say, my hat!"

"He's persuasive, Sir John, and cunning. Once inside your house he'll case it, that's police jargon, for a visit later. Perhaps you would make an appointment with him if he calls and contact us. We'd appreciate your cooperation."

"No problem, Inspector, always glad to be of service."

After half an hour I would telephone Sir John.

"Hello, Sir John Bigsby-Edwards speaking."

"Ah, it-is-a Sir John. Good. Ma name eez Meester Elio."

"Good God!"

"Sir John?"

And so the conversation would proceed, with a nervous Sir John, completely taken in, or so we thought. It was wicked of us, unbelievable, but it worked.

Another favourite gag involved calling someone to ask how much cable there was from their telephone to the wall point. Usually the victim would comply and measure. We would then tell them that they should have much more than that, and that we had yards of it at our end, so would they mind pulling at the wire to get some of ours? You would be amazed how many people said, "Certainly." After a few moments the phone would go dead.

Once we brought in a French-speaking friend called Gerald to phone a bicycle shop at Herne Hill, which was owned by an elderly Frenchman called Don Louis. Gerald rang him up and told him in French that his call-up papers had come through for enlistment in the French Foreign Legion. A blusterous Mr Louis declared, in perfect French, that he was Welsh, and there must be some mistake.

We once managed to get the entire inhabitants of an old people's home to stand in carpet slippers in the middle of the dining room. We told them the walls had become live due to a massive electricity earthing fault, and they had to wait for the all-clear from the Electricity Board to say that it was safe to touch them again.

A friendlier gag involved telling the recipients that they had won "ten minutes of serenity". We would then play them a piece of classical music, such as something from *Swan Lake*, or one of the more soothing passages from Holst's *The Planet*s. This was well-intentioned. We had dozens of satisfied customers.

We also rang Dennis Wheatley regularly, to ask him how his new book was getting on. He got to know us well and gave us updates. He guessed we were kids. It was incredible to be able to speak to him, he was always friendly, but sometimes one of the household got to the phone first and told us that Mr Wheatley did not take personal calls. Wheatley learned that we were amateur writers, and he sent me an autographed copy of a rare pamphlet he had written during the war.

It may be hard to believe, but Sir Winston

Churchill was listed in the telephone book. He had been Malcolm's hero. We often rang him for a quick conversation and when he became terminally ill we used to speak to Lady Churchill, passing on get well wishes. If the Queen's number had been listed I believe Malcolm would have suggested that we rung that too. There were many other telephone gags, some of which were too outrageous to relate here. It was all very irresponsible, but we had fun, and when my father received a huge phone bill, Malcolm and I were banned from the phone for a long time afterwards.

Robbed of access to the telephone, Malcolm and I were forced out on to the streets. We teamed up with John Yates and pursued adventures through the back gardens of south London.

There was no villainy involved. We simply wanted to experience the adventures that we read about in thrillers. Firstly, we would find a deserted side street. Next, we would climb over the back garden wall of the first house in the street. The object was for us to get into the back garden of the last house. This could sometimes entail us climbing over fifty or more fences. We had to watch for dogs, people bringing in washing, old ladies putting out cats. It was harmless and I suppose it was pointless, but to us it was dangerous and exciting.

On several occasions, Malcolm went overboard. The influence of Dennis Wheatley's characters had spread so far into his system that the real world and the imaginary became indistinguishable. Encouraged by *The Forbidden Territory*, Malcolm bought a fur papenka – a Russian fur hat. He already had the walking stick and pipe, to these he added a monocle and a fur coat. Oh yes, and a false moustache.

I didn't bother with most of the secret agent props, but I did get a walking stick to keep him company. We convinced ourselves that we were special agents, and zigzagged an undercover route across the rooftops of the local blocks of flats where Malcolm lived.

Sometimes the same escapades would occur at the allotment, off Birkbeck Place. One evening we tried to dramatize the adventure by involving Roger Fletcher, telling him that we believed that there was an undercover spy ring operating from a potting shed. He didn't believe us.

Roger Fletcher was a school friend of Malcolm's. He was, like the rest of his family, over six feet tall. He wore spectacles, walked with a greater stoop than Malcolm, and he had huge ears that looked like a pair of kites.

Roger's father was a policeman whose job was to guard the Queen Mother. He spoke in a deep West Country accent and always told Malcolm and me that we were scrawny objects. He was forever shouting at Roger to, "Turn those damn Kinks down!" (The Kinks were a sixties pop group.)

Roger's mother (who was the chief supervisor at Woolworths), his sister and twelve-year-old kid brother were also over six feet tall. Roger was useful when I wanted to see an X-rated film. An X-rated film could only be seen by persons over sixteen. I would be squeezed between Roger, John and Malcolm, and moving together quickly gave me an illusion of height. We managed to get in to most horror films with Roger, except when my age was challenged and Malcolm threatened to sue the cinema chain. This usually put the manager's back up. (My father once got me into an X-rated film by telling the manager I was a jockey.)

Roger had always been a challenge to us. He lived on the top floor of a block near Tulse Hill. Malcolm and I regularly played the Waddington's strategy game Risk, with a small group of friends in his bedroom. (Risk games were impassioned.) When we left at the end of the night we would set ourselves the challenge of trying to remove some large item of furniture without any of the Fletcher family noticing. We once got Mr Fletcher's armchair downstairs, but when the lift door opened we were faced by Roger himself.

Our greatest achievement was when we got the fridge to the third floor.

HARRISON MARKS, SPACE ROCKETS AND SMOKESTACK LIGHTNING

I noticed that the bed in the sitting room was pulled down much earlier and more often than usual. My father began to appear in the late afternoons when I got home from school, having closed up the shows at Battersea. He had started to look flushed and tired. Although he was reluctant to talk about it, it was becoming obvious that the Festival Gardens were grating on his nerves. Business was very bad – for everybody – and the move across to sideshows had given him staffing problems he never dreamed he would have to cope with. Teenage boys and girls and the general pressure of "Swinging London Life" were more than he could handle. The freedom, fashion, the dancing and the general attitudes were threats to order. Hair was his biggest problem. He had always been a short back and sides person. While I had grudgingly allowed this haircut to be inflicted on me when younger, I now resisted it. I had average length hair, but in his eyes I looked like Rapunzel.

I loved the sixties era and everything it stood for: the flamboyance and colour, the music and the hype. Every Friday evening on the television, a pop music programme announced that, "The weekend starts here!" *Ready Steady Go* became a pulse for pop culture, but it also tried to generate new directions and ideas for British teenagers rather than just bounce them back. The show went out before a live, dancing audience and was immediate, topical and played the kind of music I felt drawn towards.

My father found it impossible to sit through this programme without making derisory comments. All the popular groups, including the Beatles – who were rapidly becoming a cult – were featured. But the Beatles were of less interest to me, then. I thought they didn't stand comparison with the Rolling Stones and R&B.

Many British bands were experimenting with the rhythm and blues sound. There was Manfred Mann, the Downliners Sect, John Mayall, Them, the Zombies, Alex Harvey, Alexis Korner, Graham Bond Organisation and the wonderful Yardbirds, from which came Eric Clapton, Jeff Beck and Jimmy Page. The Rolling Stones, however, made my father's blood pressure soar. TV close-ups of Mick Jagger would force my father out of the house to the Tulse Hill Hotel. The dog was leashed up and the pair of them would disappear.

Having my own bedroom and my own record

player meant that I could now play records whenever I wanted to. The bedroom became my lair.

I continued to work at weekends at Battersea Park, which earned me enough money to buy records, and I was beginning to collect seriously rather than casually.

At school Bob West had started to learn to play the harmonica in the style of the American blues players. He was good, too. He often called round to my house and brought Sonny Boy Williamson records with him.

One day he brought a special forty-five rpm single. It had a yellow label, produced by a company I had never heard of – Pye. The title of the song was strange too: "Smokestack Lightning", by Howlin' Wolf. Bob explained that it was a reissue; the record was first released on the American Chess label in March 1956. He'd just heard it and had bought it immediately. With a shrug, I put the record on the player and listened carefully.

Howlin' Wolf was an appropriate name. Almost indecipherable lyrics were growled. But it was an incredible song: raw, dynamic, gutsy and magnificently unpolished. And it had soul, and a sense of hopelesness that, for some reason, appealed to me.

I went out the next day and bought his LP.

Some of his lyrics were extraordinarily grotesque and outrageous – I loved them.

First thing in the morning,
Just before I rise,
You lie there rolling your bloodshot eyes,
I'm leaving this morning.

And

I asked for water
You gave me gasoline.

This music touched a nerve within me. It was my first real introduction to the blues, rather than through the cover versions of English bands. I was taken by the dynamic of the original. Homesick James, Robert Johnson, Elmore James, Muddy Waters, Jimmy Witherspoon, Big Bill Broonzy – the list was endless. These singers were mostly poor, unheard of. When "Little Red Rooster" (recorded by the Stones) went to the top of the charts it was the Stones who received the fortune and fame, although it was one of the Wolf's songs.

Stacks of rhythm and blues records grew beside my record player. I breathed the music, and at school – with the help of our art teacher, Mr Paul – Bob, Daisy and I set up a blues club, meeting at lunch times to listen to records in the art studio.

A kid at school's brother had an electric guitar for sale, and it was going cheap. It was my opportunity to try to learn how to play like the musicians who were becoming my heroes. I managed to persuade my father to give me a sub against the next two months' weekend work, and I bought the guitar. An intensive period of practice followed.

Meanwhile, my mother was still trying to inculcate the importance of an academic education. School work and a passion for records and learning the guitar had taken over from writing fiction, although I still read avidly. I was also seeing less of

Malcolm and John. Their main concern was now the problem of How to Pick Up Girls. Since my hormones were a couple of years behind theirs, I was temporarily abandoned.

Their pick-up techniques never seemed too successful. Sometimes these pick-ups were attempted in the local park, on other occasions they came to the funfair, hoping that my connections would get them free rides, an extra ace up their sleeve to entice lucky ladies.

I suppose my own first real encounter with sex was when Robin Hodges, a boy in my class, gave me a Harrison Marks pocket book of "photographic art studies". The "study" in question was of a fairly famous sixties model, June Palmer. Opening the pages my head started to swim and I felt the earth tremble. I thought she looked amazing. I took the book home.

The next morning a mysterious rash appeared on the side of my face. It was my first spot, the beginnings of adolescent acne (which plagued me as I grew up). I remembered the June Palmer photo book and wondered if this was the cause.

It did not take me long for my new interests to catch up with Malcolm's and we started to meet up again. Our teen years were spent going to lots of parties. Malcolm had started to go out with a girl called Sarah, who he had met at a local youth club. They married eventually (and later divorced). The relationship with Sarah meant access to an entire bevy of beauties – her school friends.

Sarah went to Mary Datchelor, a grammar school near Forest Hill. Mary Datchelor girls always seemed to be having parties, and at a party given by a girl named Eileen Prue, a girl with incredibly long hair grabbed me and put her tongue down my throat. I saw stars. I thought her tongue had reached down to the insides of my toes.

After the party I was certain that I was in love. The girl's name was Jennifer. The trouble was that Jennifer was going out with somebody else. She felt torn, poor creature, so we went out secretly until the situation got too difficult: *people were talking*. We had been seen together at the cinema, canoodling in the front row at a Hammer horror film.

I later learned that the same Eileen who had thrown the party liked me. But there was one small (or tall) problem and this seemed important to most girls – she was taller than me. I didn't mind though, and neither did Eileen once we started to see each other. When we said good night in the hallway, I stood on tiptoes, or she crouched down slightly.

My father was now viewing me with sidelong glances. I was obviously growing into a typical modern rebellious youth, the kind that locked themselves in their rooms with loud rock and roll and jazz records. His health had started to suffer. He was becoming tired and short of breath. His visits home were more frequent, and I was having to take on an even greater managerial role at Battersea, something that I guess he was grateful for. It was as if we rode on the same see-saw and my end of the plank was rising. His life had been one of performance; but the showman era, and that of older style Variety, no longer fitted. Battersea Park and the blues band that we had just formed provided me with a perfect vehicle for my own style of show-manship.

I discovered real sex, ironically, through my father's shows. Shirley and Sheila were two girls from Yorkshire who had travelled to London in search of the Bright Lights and Big City. They were step-sisters, from a mining family, and looked and dressed exactly alike. They came to Battersea Park one night when I was demonstrating the Invisible Ray.

They looked quite stunning, like a pair of dolls, in long black and white shiny macs, tiny mini-skirts and knee-length white Kinky boots. Their hair was teased up at the back, and they wore heavy mascara, thick eye-liner and bright red lipstick.

I demonstrated the Invisible Ray to a small audience. Shirley and Sheila stayed after the show, and the young employee who was taking tickets for me, Fred, chatted them up. Fred was an East Ender, older than me, with a good gift of the gab.

Shirley kept making cow eyes in my direction. I wondered if she was trying to be funny, but Fred assured me that she was "interested". I found this hard to believe. You will have to picture this: I had National Health spectacles, spots, and I think my jeans flapped above my ankles. I probably had my school shoes on too.

Shirley *was* interested though, and Fred and I walked the sisters to the bus-stop when the fair closed. She told me she was nineteen, I lied and told her I was sixteen (I was, in fact, fourteen and looked younger).

When we stopped at the bus-stop, Shirley

explained that they had to go on to work. It turned
out that she worked a late shift in an East End night
club. She was an escort for the club clientele.

Shirley came back to the fair the next night, just
to see me. I found this behaviour disconcerting and
strange. I wasn't used to this at all. She declared
true love after two weeks and we started to go out
together. Shirley declared that if I ever "chucked
her" she would throw herself off Waterloo Bridge.

My parents disapproved when they learned of the
liaison, but did not interfere.

I brought Shirley over to Malcolm's house to meet
Malcolm. Mrs Saunders was astonished. Shirley was
decked out in more and more expensive jewellery
every time I saw her. We must have looked a strange
pair.

Shirley wanted me to spend the night with her. I
told my father that I'd been invited to an all-night
party as my parents wouldn't allow me to spend the
night away from home. I knew my father smelt a rat.
Instead, I crept out of the house at four o'clock one
morning and caught the first early tube train and
bus to Islington, where the sisters had their bedsit.
Shirley opened the door with half-awake eyes. She
slept in a large fold-out double bed; her sister was on
the floor in a sleeping bag. I climbed into the sofa
bed. I think I kept my trousers on, although I was
immediately told to take them off.

The experience was a disaster. The earth didn't
move a centimetre, and I wondered what the fuss
was all about. It hadn't lasted long. Feeling acutely
embarrassed I made my apologies and said something crass like, "It was the power of lurrrve, so

strong that I could not hold myself back." I felt that was what an Ian Fleming character would have said.

A week or so later, when I suspected that certain important parts of me were not as they should be, I clumsily told my father about the entanglement. All hell broke loose. This did not help his blood pressure one bit. He kept walking up and down the corridor of the flat repeating, "I knew it, I damn well knew it, tell me again what you did!"

That was the most embarrassing bit, explaining what I did.

I went over it again. Then he walked up and down the corridor and asked me to go over it again but in greater detail.

I was shuffled off to the family GP that evening, who also asked me to explain, "in my own words", what it was that I had done. He gave me a letter, which I had to take to the Special Clinic at King's College Hospital. He told me that I didn't need to make an appointment.

I went the following morning, with my geography books under my arm to revise for a test. I walked into the reception area at the hospital and handed them the letter. A lady behind the counter stared at me as though I had received orders for a secret mission, and leant forward. She pushed a folded sheet into my hand and whispered, "Here's a map of how to get there. The instructions are inside. It's round the back."

I felt as if I were one of Dennis Wheatley's characters. The sheet referred to the "A Block", which, according to the map, was located right at the back of the hospital, a door of shame. I wondered whether

I should have worn a long dirty raincoat.

I followed the instructions on the map but did manage to get lost. I ended up popping into a hospital side door. I simply asked the way in a loud unconcerned voice.

The clinic staff were friendly, but I must have been an unusual sight, sitting there with O level Physical Geography on my lap. A male nurse kept strutting up and down the corridor, as my father had done. He recited passages from the Bible in a loud effeminate voice. He stopped in front of me and asked me how old I was. I told him, to which he responded by sucking through his teeth and tutting until I thought his teeth would fall out. He returned to the Bible.

As it turned out, there was nothing wrong with me. I had merely had an allergic reaction. Shirley only rang me once afterwards. I received a goodbye letter; she had met somebody else who worked in a menswear shop. I was never sure, but I believe my father had intercepted one of her phone calls and told her to stop ringing. Something that was said at Battersea Park by Fred indicated that he might know more than he let on. I think Shirley had been told my real age.

When Battersea closed down for the winter I had to find another kind of Saturday work. Usually I worked at a local wallpaper and paint shop. If business wasn't going well I was laid off. A regular job was important; it was my only way of getting any money.

Other attempts to find work had been disastrous. Gardening, which I neither understood nor liked, was a failure. A car-cleaning venture with Malcolm did not run smoothly. He always ripped me off and took a larger share of "our fee" because he owned the bucket and sponge and the John Bull printing outfit to make our business cards.

I replied to an advert in a newsagent that said "Young boy wanted for cleaning duties." The address was local. It was a strange and large house, divided into lots of bedsit rooms, almost like a hostel. The waxen-faced man who answered the door and insisted I chatted to him over a cup of tea explained that these were "rooms for men" (whatever that meant). The conversation switched to whether I was interested in modelling for photographs. (*Hello*, I thought.) When I asked him what he meant he pulled out a drawer full of photographs of slim pale boys in various nude statuesque poses. One boy was wearing a pair of goat horns on his head and another a pair of antlers. I wondered what on earth this was all about. I was astonished.

"Not my thing, mate," I said, in as deep and gruff a voice as I could muster. "My mate Malcolm might be interested though. I'll get him to call you."

I gulped my tea, made my excuses and left.

Having rejected the offer of a "modelling" career, I got a Saturday job working at the local library. My father, however, was no longer able to take on any winter work when Battersea closed down. His blood pressure had become very serious indeed and he constantly complained of feeling unwell. His income tax returns, the receipts and paperwork, had been piled in a corner of the sitting room for months. At the close of the season the Festival Gardens had been barely alive.

The blues had begun to loom larger in my life. Getting into the music was easy – it provided expression and escape. I could never entirely understand the argument for blues and jazz being valid only as music from the slums. If what you do comes from the heart, then it will be real, no matter what your background or where you come from. The blues was becoming real to me.

Although not poor by the measure of real poverty, we were now finding survival a struggle. The only certain income came from my mother, who had got a job in the Civil Service. A shadow of sadness hung over our lives. My father was haunted by ghosts – the image of the slow death of show business as he had known it, the decline in live Variety. The old values were changing. I think that was what made my father ill. A pharmacist's array of tablets now stood on the tea trolley.

I was woken one morning at five o'clock, and told by my mother to "come quickly, your father's collapsed". I didn't understand what she meant by "collapsed". How could someone "collapse"? It sounded dramatic.

My father had fallen on his way back to bed from the bathroom. My mother had heard a crash and found him lying across the glass coffee table. At first she was worried about the cut on his head, but then she realized that he couldn't stand and he looked vague. He was a big man and it was difficult for the two of us to get him back into the bed, but we did it.

He recovered from the stroke, but he was weak and depressed and seemed to have aged.

Dispirited by the relative failure of the sideshows and all the staffing problems, he decided to install a couple of illusory rides for the next season. My mother and I wished he would give up the business altogether. I feared it was killing him, but he was a stubborn man, and something inside him, a love/hate relationship, wouldn't allow him to let the Festival Gardens go.

Although he suffered two more strokes that year, he struggled on and made a deal with the company that produced these rides. The plan had not been properly worked out; he told my mother very little and it was "none of my business".

He got involved with a character called Bill, who often hung about the fair. Bill was given the job of managing the new rides on a fifty-fifty split. Bill was an interesting character. He was about forty years old and often sported a Mohican hairstyle, and this was before punks had ever been thought of. He was a hard character and had the pedigree to match. But he was likeable. He had worked in the circus as a rodeo stunt man, and had also got by doing "a bit of this and a bit of that", and singing country and western.

We opened the next season with the Speed Boat and the Space Rocket. The principle of both rides was the same. The Space Rocket was a small cabin with a large front window and half a dozen side windows. The "passengers" sat on bench seats beside these windows. A recording would give a countdown to "blast off". Suddenly the cabin shook and lunged forward. Views of planets and stars passed by. And that was it. The cabin didn't really go anywhere; rollers of outer space scenery, painted on screens, went past by the windows giving the illusion of movement.

It was clever, but limited. It was more a younger kid's thing than a general ride. Sensation-seeking, hard-to-please Mods and Rockers emerged with disappointed faces.

Near our pitch was a carousel. It was called the Gallopers. A fairground organ thumped out well-known melodies day and night. Gold and silver horses with blonde manes rose and fell as punters were carried round and round. I used to stand in the doorway of our shows and watch the people ride the carousel. It had always been a symbol of the fairground. But now, kids with Beatles jackets and mop-head hair rode the wooden horses. Mini-skirted girls sat at the rear wearing "fab gear", beehive hairdos and huge earrings. They would cling on to their boyfriends' waists and scream with excitement.

When I first came to Battersea, the carousel was as bright and shiny as a new car, the paintwork gleaming and fresh. Now I noticed that like much of the other equipment and rides in the funfair, signs of wear, of neglect, of decay, were beginning to show.

As my father's illness grew worse, so the affairs of the funfair became more distant. He didn't care about the place any more. My mother was beginning to worry about what might be going on there, so I left the library to work alongside Bill at weekends and some evenings. Additional staff appeared at the shows: men with long drawn faces, heavily shadowed jowels and certain looks in their eyes. I recall one

man called Jim, who constantly referred to "his little spell away". The Space Rocket was becoming a
reunion venue for old lags.

One evening a stocky, bustling, moustached man
with gold earrings turned up at the shows. He
was a seasoned fairground worker called Lee, a professional con man, part-time burglar, and a
fairground attraction in his own right. "The man
with a hundred earrings"; he had them everywhere,
as he showed us. He was an all-round villain and he
never stopped grinning. He claimed to have burgled
the rich and famous, and I believed him.

Lee got on well with Bill, and with me too. I knew
he had to be watched with an eagle eye, but I
couldn't help liking him. The entire situation at
Battersea was becoming crazy, a vein of black comedy ran through everything that we did.

As I was about to sit my A levels, in the summer
of '68, my father went into hospital again. One day
I received a telephone call from the park manager at
the Festival Gardens. I knew that they were unhappy
about Bill.

It turned out that Bill had lost his temper the previous evening, after a row with a senior park official.
He had closed the shows down and gone off in a
huff. I learned that this often happened, and the
midgets who ran the House of Laughter Crazy Mirrors show next door were feeling intimidated by the
Hell's Kitchen gangs that clustered outside the
Space Rocket. It was a serious problem because we
were contractually obliged to keep the shows running at all times.

After a discussion with my mother, we decided

that Bill had to go. The entire arrangement had been made on trust, and Bill was abusing that trust. I was going to have to take over. I agreed to go down to Battersea and tell Bill to pack his bags. My mother would speak to him on the phone to reinforce this.

We never told my father.

If asked to undertake this now, I think I would be very wary. Some of the men that hung about the shows were dangerous characters, not to be messed with ... but at the age of eighteen?

When I arrived at Battersea it looked as though all the ex-inmates of HM prisons Brixton and Pentonville had taken over the place. I paused and stared at the crowd before approaching them. It was funny. I wondered if my grandfather was revolving in his grave, probably at a hundred miles an hour.

I held my breath. Then I told them all that they would have to leave – and to my amazement, they did. I explained the position to Bill. He was annoyed, that was all. I was surprised at his reaction, but I was glad that he accepted it without any fuss. Perhaps he had grown tired of it himself. Bill had a certain dignity about him, as did all the others. But the business couldn't continue in that way. I still have a soft spot for all of them.

The world was threatening to cave in on me. I seemed to have commitments and problems everywhere: my exams were looming; I had joined a band on the other side of London and was playing regularly; my father's condition was getting worse, although he was now back at home, and I had the family business on my shoulders. I coped, however, and managed to restaff quickly, conducting detailed interviews. I would call in on the shows in the evenings and some weekends. After all, there was only the rest of the summer season to contend with, and I had a feeling that this was going to be the last.

A few weeks later I got home from school to find that the ambulance had already called and they had taken my father again.

A hastily scribbled note from my mother lay on the living-room table. The put-up wall bed was still down. The sheets were crumpled, thrown to one side, and a pile of ironing had been hastily ransacked. It had been a hurried departure.

Mother's note named a hospital that I hadn't heard of. The address was somewhere in the middle of London, not Balham or Tooting where he was usually sent. This was a new place. The note said she'd ring this evening to let me know how everything was going.

I was due to play the next night at a club on the other side of west London. I'd left a message with our roadie, a John Peel look-alike nicknamed Orange, that I couldn't make the rehearsal. They knew about my father.

After reading my mother's note and tidying up, I made myself some tea and went and sat in my bedroom. I felt cold and alone.

Our band took their name from the Chicago loop district: the South Side Express. Every member was an East Ender, and I had to make the trek across the city to rehearse in an evening institute classroom.

Nobody at school knew my co-musicians. Daisy and Keith laughed at our name.

"South Side Express! What do you mean South Side? You're not black, you don't live in any tin hut in Mississippi. You get food in your belly. You've never met the blues."

I wondered whether they were right.

I hid myself away in my room trying to imitate the guitar riffs from John Mayall records, or, if I wanted the roots, Homesick James and Johnny Shines. But it was always just imitating. Borrowing. Maybe stealing.

My mother returned home later that evening looking exhausted. She had telephoned earlier and explained that my father was very ill indeed this time, and that there was no point in my going over to the hospital. Not yet. They wouldn't let me see him.

I mentioned cancelling the gig we had tomorrow night, but my mother said I should keep the date. There was something insistent about the maxim "the show must go on"; it had been instilled in me since I could walk. It was in their blood, it was in my blood. I said that Orange would drop me off at the hospital afterwards. I could finish my set early.

The club where we were playing was enormous – a cavern of a place, empty and depressing, with broad DJ-suited bouncers on the doors. Gradually, during the evening, the space filled up.

We kicked off, as always, with a mixture of popular stuff, dance material. It wasn't until the middle set that we played rhythm and blues. That was our time, the audience could like it or lump it. The third set was a combination of the two.

I hadn't played much in the opening numbers.

There were two of us who shared lead, and since I now mainly played bottleneck, my style was particular and restricted. I never played on all our numbers.

The other members of the group had left me alone; I'd been unusually (but understandably) quiet. Orange had begun to realize that this time the situation was serious. I had telephoned the hospital from the pub opposite the club before we went on stage. I was passed over to the ward sister. Usually I was told that he was "comfortable" by an ordinary staff nurse. Now I was told that, "there is no change in your father's serious condition."

During the first break I telephoned the hospital again.

I was passed on to another ward sister. She sounded kindly and sympathetic, with a softer voice than was usual. She repeated the same message as before, but then she added, "He's seriously ill, you know, love."

I felt sad and strange. I wasn't even at home, I don't think I knew where I was. No tears came. Somehow I had toughened.

When I got back to the club the others had opened with an old Albert King number, "Crosscut Saw". I stood in the doorway where the bouncers had their table and stared across the dance floor of three girls to every boy. The acoustics were dreadful, the band sounded amateurish.

I walked slowly over to the stage and climbed up on to the platform steps from the rear. Then, I did something unusual. I'd never developed a stage act – these were far cries from Michael Jackson days – but I would strut up and down out front with Bill, the other guitarist, and sometimes do the odd vocal. Tonight I pulled an old canvas-covered chair alongside the Marshall amplifier stack at the back. I sat down and rested the guitar on my knee. With a nod to our drummer I led straight into a slow twelve bar number. The others followed.

It was improvised. It was our time.

My guitar solo must have gone on for ages, I don't know how long exactly. Nobody signalled me to stop. Time stood still. The kids in the audience simply smooched, slow-danced and went with the mood.

I think we played slow twelve-bars for most of the set.

I was an "OK" guitarist – nothing to crow about – but the guitar breaks this night were probably the best I had ever played. The notes came from another place. Everything that had been pent up inside, pushed down and hardened simply to help me get through each day, came out.

Then, I made a special request to the others. We played "Smokestack Lightning".

I may have just been from south London, living in a first floor flat with my parents, but that night Daisy and Keith were wrong. I didn't need to be from a Chicago slum to play the blues.

AFTERWARDS

The summer of '68 passed like a fleeting dream. My father died that summer during a heat-wave. We didn't want him to live any more; he had become so ill and his dignity was fading fast. His death was sad, but it also brought with it a great relief. He was fifty-nine.

I had just finished sitting my A levels. I forgot the South Side Express and began to wind down the Festival Gardens business. I decided to postpone going to university or college for a year, that was assuming I was going to be offered a place.

I returned to Battersea Park towards the end of the season to sort out the staff and the bits and pieces that had been hidden away in old trunks for years. The funfair was almost deserted. The love and peace and vital messages of the sixties were looking tarnished. Drug-taking had reached epidemic level, and the fair was known as a place to pick up stuff. As the carousel turned all you saw were teenagers, bleary-eyed with alternative dreams. The rides boys, who collected the money, had pale blue mosaic bruises scattered among the amateurish tattoos on their arms.

The sounds of the sixties – the Beatles, the Small

Faces, the Stones – were everywhere. They flowed from transistor radios, from the park public address system. It all crashed into the seediness of the "Festival Pleasure Gardens" – now the name seemed ironic.

The year that followed was a mixture of new experiences. We pulled out of Battersea Park, and a few years later the place was closed down. There was a boom in the blues that year. Another friend of our group at school, Danny Kirwan, joined Fleetwood Mac, who leapt up the charts with "Albatross". Danny invited us all to the Albert Hall concert, which was sensational.

Danny Kirwan, Jeremy Spencer and Peter Green all left later, each suffering from the strains of so much so quickly. Fleetwood Mac went on to become an AOR (Adult-Oriented Rock) band, and settled in California. Recently Mick Fleetwood, the gentle and charismatic drummer who lent his name to the band, was visibly moved when the band was described as a "group of friends who had been together a very long time".

I continued playing slide guitar with many different scratch bands: Shaky Vick's Bluesband, the Dynaflow Blues Band, the Nighthawks and a later version of the Spencer Davis Group. I had never been particularly good, but in the two years before I went to university, I got better. It had something to do with playing from the heart.

I went off to Manchester University in September 1969. My mother couldn't believe the irony of my returning to the place I had started from – back to the gibbons and the seals.

I went to look around the Belle Vue site one cold winter's afternoon. The place had become a wasteland. Like Battersea Park, it had died. The echoes of circus excitement, the roar of my father's motorcycles and the cries of the zoo animals were clear in my memory.

The gibbons and the seals.

I could hear them, they were singing the blues:
"Smokestack Lightning"?
Perhaps.

ORDINARY SEAMAN

John Gordon

Towards the end of the Second World War, the teenage John Gordon served as an Ordinary Seaman on board a minesweeper. He had some harrowing experiences; coming to terms with the peculiar traditions, practices and language of the Navy was a trial in itself... This fascinating memoir is his story.

PIG IGNORANT

Nicholas Fisk

"Pig ignorant" is how Nicholas Fisk describes his sixteen-year-old self, growing up in the 1940s. Living and working in London during the Blitz, he spent his evenings playing jazz in Soho and trying not to notice that the world was at war around him. This vivid memoir is his story.

YESTERDAY

Adèle Geras

When, as a teenager, Adèle Geras visited Oxford for the first time, she fell in love with it at once. She went up to the university in 1963, the year President Kennedy was assassinated and the Beatles released their first LP. Joining the theatre crowd, she soon found herself involved in dramas on and off the stage. This entertaining "Sixties" memoir is her story.

BACKTRACK

Peter Hunt

"Our Correspondent in Hereford last night informed us of another shocking railway catastrophe. A train was derailed near the village of Elmcote with terrible results..." The Times, Friday, September 3rd, 1915

When Jack and Rill meet one summer, they discover that they both had great uncles involved in an old and still unexplained railway crash. So who better to try to find out what really happened?

"A smashing mystery/thriller... If you like ideas as well as action, *Backtrack* is for you." *Weekend*

"Imaginative ... a nice astringent variant on the boy-girl motif."
The Observer

THE FLITHER PICKERS

Theresa Tomlinson

"Northern sea, silver sea,
Bring my daddy home to me,
Hush the waves and still the sea,
And bring my daddy back to me."

Life is hard for the fisher folk living and working on the north-east coast at the turn of the century. The men face death daily in the often stormy sea, while the women, the flither pickers, gather bait from the shore. Children who are too young to work, like Liza Welford, are supposed to go to school. But what have books and sums to do with a child of the sea?

Based on real events, this novel is illustrated with black-and-white photographs of the period by the celebrated Frank Meadow Sutcliffe.

"A gritty, touching novel of the North Yorkshire coast." *The Guardian*

THE BURNING BABY
AND OTHER GHOSTS
John Gordon

The glowing ashes turned again and then, from the centre, there arose a small entity, a little shape of fire. It had a small torso, small limbs, and a head of flame. And it walked.

A teenage girl disappears mysteriously a few days before bonfire night; two youths out skating see something grisly beneath the ice; an elderly spinster feeds her young charge to the eels... Unnatural or violent death are at the heart of these five supernatural tales, in which wronged spirits seek to exact a terrible and terrifying retribution on the living. Vivid as fire, chilling as ice, their stories will haunt you.

"All the stories include hauntingly memorable apparitions... A major collection." *Ramsey Campbell, Necrofile*

MORE WALKER PAPERBACKS
For You to Enjoy

**Walker Paperbacks are available from most booksellers. They are also available
by post: just tick the titles you want, fill in the form below and send it to
Walker Books Ltd, PO Box 11, Falmouth, Cornwall TR10 9EN.**

Please send a cheque or postal order and allow the following for postage and packing:
UK & BFPO – £1.00 for first book, plus 50p for second book and
plus 30p for each additional book to a maximum charge of £3.00.
Overseas and Eire Customers – £2.00 for first book, plus £1.00 for second book,
plus 50p per copy for each additional book.
Prices are correct at time of going to press, but are subject to change without notice.

Name _____

Address _____

_____